POLAR YETI

AND THE BEASTS OF PREHISTORY

MATTHEW DENNION

SEVERED PRESS
HOBART TASMANIA

POLAR YETI AND THE BEASTS OF PREHISTORY

PROLOGUE

Antarctica

The cold wind whipped across the barren ice as several penguins wandered around looking for the optimal spot to build a nest. Jun-Tuk pulled his seal skin coat tighter over his torso. He was a member of the Quinic tribe. He was used to the harsh cold that was a constant fact of life to the people who lived just above the South Pole. The old man shivered, but it was not the sub-zero winds that blew around him that caused his body to shake. He was shivering out of fear and concern for his daughter, Shunu. Two weeks ago, the ten-month period had passed since the Quinic's last offering to the Yeti. The Yeti had returned to the village looking for one of the Quinic's young women to be offered to him. Against Jun-Tuk's wishes, Shunu had insisted on offering herself to the monster. Jun-Tuk's wife had died long ago and Shunu was the only family that he had left. Now that two weeks had passed, Jun-Tuk and the hunters were waiting at the mid-way point between the village and the pass that led to the valley between the mountains. They were all hoping to see the Yeti return with Shunu alive and well in his clutches.

The wind whipped a gust of snow off the ground and into Jun-Tuk's face, causing the old man to close his eyes. With his eyes closed, Jun-Tuk recalled the history of the beast that held his beloved daughter's life in his clawed hands. When Jun-Tuk was a young man, the Yeti had first appeared outside of his village. The wild-man was a giant who was covered in thick white fur. The Yeti walked on two legs but its body was thick and far more powerful than any human. He face was long with blood red eyes, while his mouth was filled with sharp, dagger-like teeth.

The beast wandered into the village where he began tearing down the seal skin tents that the villagers' lived in. Many of the village's hunters ran out to try and slay the beast, but their spears were unable to pierce the Yeti's thick fur and dense muscles. The Yeti rampaged through village until he found one of the young women hiding inside of a tent. The Yeti picked up the young woman and wandered off into the tundra with her. Several of the hunters tried to the follow the creature, but he was large and he moved too fast for them to keep up with. After chasing the Yeti for nearly two days, the hunters tracked the monster to a valley pass between the huge mountains to the west of their tribe. The valley pass was filled with large and jagged boulders. Once the hunters climbed to the top of the pass, they looked into the valley and they saw that it was filled with demons. At the sight of the demons, the hunters were forced to abandon their quest and to return to the village.

Once the hunters had returned to the village, the members of the tribe had assumed that the Yeti had devoured the woman. The day after abduction, the chief of the tribe presided over a funeral for the girl. She was honored and each member of the tribe provided some manner of compensation to the woman's father for the loss of his daughter.

For several months, the elders of the tribe met with the chief and they discussed what actions would be taken if the Yeti was to return again. The hunters made several suggestions on new ways to attack to the wild-man. The tribe's spiritual leaders, however, felt strongly that the Yeti was not an animal but a god. They contended that if the Yeti was to be worshipped by the Quinic that he would no longer attack the tribe and that he would even protect them from the demons in the valley.

Ten months had passed since the abduction and the debate was still continuing as to the nature of the Yeti and how to deal with him. The spiritual leaders continued to insist that the Yeti was a god and the hunters still felt that he was a beast that could be killed. They were inside the chief's tent when they heard the roar of the Yeti. Once more, the beast searched the village until he found a young woman that he grabbed and returned to the valley with. Once more, a funeral was held for the young woman and her family.

Sixteen days after the second woman had been abducted, there was great commotion in the center of the village. The chief and the tribal elders exited their tent to see the entire tribe gathered around a single person. The chief made his way to the center of the gathered people to see the woman who had been abducted two weeks earlier being hugged by her father.

Like everyone else in the tribe, the chief was amazed to see that the woman was still alive. He embraced the girl and then ordered food, water, and new clothes to be brought to her. Once the woman was comfortable and refreshed, the chief asked her what had happened after the Yeti had abducted her.

The young woman told a story that was beyond belief. She said that the Yeti had taken her through the pass of the stone mountains that loomed far in the distance from the tribe. Once they had entered the pass, the woman was shocked to see a valley filled with monsters and demons. Several of the demons had tried to attack her but the Yeti had fought them off. The Yeti then took her to his cave where he fed the girl raw meat and provided her with water. The girl was forced to stay close the Yeti in order to keep from freezing to death.

While at first she feared that the Yeti would devour her, she soon found that the Yeti had no intention of consuming her. The Yeti simply kept the girl in his cave where she was safe from the horrors outside of it. Ten days after the Yeti had taken her, the monster picked her up and carried her back through the pass in between the mountains to the halfway point between the valley and village. He placed the young woman safely on the ground then he turned and started walking back into the valley. The chief had asked the young girl if she had seen the first woman who had been abducted but the girl replied that she had not seen her. It was assumed that the first women had displeased the Yeti and suffered his wrath.

The tribe's spiritual leaders immediately proclaimed that the woman's story indicated the Yeti was indeed a divine spirit that protected them from the horrors inside of the valley. The eldest of the spiritual leaders spoke to the chief in front of the entire tribe. "The Yeti seeks to protect us from the demons of the valley and he asks that we honor him with the offering of a young maiden when he arrives. This girl has returned alive! Surely asking one maiden to spend several moons with the Yeti is not a price beyond our ability to meet." The chief nodded in agreement with the old man. He then turned to the crowd. "Women of the Quinic, the Yeti god has chosen you to be his consorts as he battles the demons which live in the valley. It is your sacred duty to accompany the Yeti for the good of the tribe." The chief pointed to the young girl who the Yeti had recently returned. "This woman stayed close the Yeti and appeased him. In return, the Yeti protected her and our entire tribe from demons of the valley. From this day forward, when the Yeti comes, he shall be allowed to take one woman with him as payment for protecting our entire tribe from the demons which inhabit the valley. Do not fear to be taken by the Yeti. If you worship and appease him, you shall be returned to us unharmed."

From that day on, the Yeti would come to the tribe every ten months where he would find the women of the Quinic waiting for him. Roughly half of the women who were taken were returned to the halfway point between the valley and village after sixteen days had passed. The Yeti would bring the women who he chose to return to the halfway point where they would find a group of hunters that would escort them back to the village. The women who were not returned were thought to have displeased the Yeti and to have brought his wrath upon themselves.

As the years went on, less of the women were being returned to the tribe. One morning, in the tenth month from last appearance of the wild-man, the Yeti wandered into the village again. The women of the tribe had become less inclined to offer themselves to the Yeti as a sacrifice because less than half of the women who had previously been taken were returned. As such, when the Yeti came to the village, he did not find the women of the tribe waiting for him to choose one them to be his consort.

When he did not see the women waiting for him, the Yeti became enrage and attacked the village. The massive beast lifted one of the seal skins tents off the ground and threw it across the village. He was about to reach down and grab the mother and young child inside of it when one of the young woman from the village ran up to the Yeti and knelt down before him. The wild-man started at the woman for a second, and as he did so, the monster seemed to calm down. The beast reached down and gently picked the woman up in his hand. The Yeti then turned and began walking back to the valley that he inhabited.

The Quinic waited patiently for the two week period to pass to see if the woman would return alive or if she would die. The entire tribe waited at the edge of the village when the hunters embarked on their journey to retrieve the brave young maiden who had freely given herself to the rampaging Yeti. The villagers cheered with joy when they saw the hunters return with the girl.

The Yeti would continue to return to the village every ten months and each time he would take a woman from the tribe who had offered herself up to him. It seemed as if the pattern continued of the Yeti returning the women who pleased him while the women who displeased him were never seen again. The elders of the tribe urged the woman who offered themselves to the wild-man to stay near the Yeti and to try and please him so that he would return them to their loved ones.

One of hunters shouted snapping Jun-Tuk back to the present. "Look! I see the Yeti, he approaches!"

Jun-Tuk's heart leapt for joy! In cases where the woman did not return, the Yeti did not bother to leave the valley. Jun-Tuk could see his daughter in the Yeti's hand but as he looked closer, he could also see a line of red that led down the Yeti's hand and dripped onto the snow.

The Yeti walked until he was roughly one hundred yards from the hunters where he placed Shunu onto the frozen ground. The Yeti then turned and started walking back toward the mountains. Jun-Tuk ran across the ice to his daughter. He saw that she had a circular puncture wound in her abdomen that was roughly the size of a baseball. Several of the hunters rushed over and they begin to treat the girl's wound. The lead hunter had managed to stop the bleeding but he turned to Jun-Tuk with a look of remorse on his face. "I have seen wounds like this before inflicted on the men who hunt the tusked walrus. While we have stopped the blood from leaving her body, she is still bleeding inside of her stomach." He placed his hand on Jun-Tuk's shoulder. "She will join your ancestors in the spirit world within five days."

Jun-Tuk's eyes began to fill with tears. His mind was swirling with anger, fear, despair, and desperation. He could not comprehend what had occurred. Shunu had given herself to the Yeti. How could he allow harm to come to her or to harm her himself? Jun-Tuk had taught his daughter since she was a child to appease and honor the Yeti if she was ever taken by him. A thought entered the old man's mind and he turned to the hunter. "Take me to the canoes. I will take her to the continent. They will have the medicine to heal her."

The hunter shook his head. "No, Jun-Tuk. It is forbidden. Do not take her to the continent. To do so would reveal the existence of our tribe to the outside world."

Jun-Tuk stood and yelled, "She has given herself to the Yeti in order to protect our tribe! She has risked her life to protect all of us! Is it not fair to ask the tribe to put themselves in a small amount of danger to save her now?"

Jun-Tuk picked up his daughter and he began walking in the direction of the canoes. The hunter yelled, "Jun-Tuk, if you attempt to take her to the continent, you will not be allowed to rejoin the tribe! You will be an outcast!" Jun-Tuk did not answer; he simply continued to walk in the direction of the canoes.

A second hunter walked up to the leader of the group. "Should we stop him?"

The leader shook his head. "No. The journey to the continent is nearly impossible for several healthy men. For an old man to make the journey with a dying girl is impossible. We shall return to the tribe. We shall inform the elders that Shunu died a great hero at the hands of the Yeti and the Jun-Tuk died as an outcast."

CHAPTER 1

Ushuaia, Argentina

The punch connected to her chin and it felt like she had been hit in the jaw with a baseball bat. Gina Murella fell to the ground and landed flat on her back. Her head bounced off the floor hard before it finally came to a rest on the mat. Gina saw lights flashing before her eyes. She blinked several times to try and clear up her blurry vision. She was starting to regain her senses when she felt a heavy weight press down on her chest. Her eyesight cleared just in time to see a gloved fist coming at her face. Her instincts took over and she rolled her face with the punch. The blow still hurt but she had managed to avoid the worst of it. She saw another fist raise into the air and then it stopped. The woman who had been pounding on Gina climbed off her and returned to her corner.

Gina's husband, Henry, climbed into the cage and helped Gina to her feet. He half-carried her back to her corner where he slumped her down onto a stool. "That's it, babe, she nearly took your head off with that last punch."

Gina took out her mouth piece as the bun that her long blonde hair was done in came undone. "No way, I am not stopping. I am finishing this fight."

Henry pointed at the fighter across the ring. "She's ten years younger than you and she is a full-time professional fighter! You are a professor of anthropology who trains in MMA to stay in shape." Henry pointed across the cage, "Look at her. She has at least twenty pounds of muscle on you. She is a freaking Amazon for crying out loud! She is going to hurt you and for what? To prove that you're tough? To blow off some steam?"

Gina turned to her husband with an utter look of frustration. "We have been down here for nine months and made two trips to Antarctica without finding a single shred of evidence that this reported lost tribe that we have heard about exists. If we don't find something soon, our funding is going to be pulled and we both may lose our jobs. Maybe it's time I started looking to switch careers and become a professional fighter."

Henry shrugged. "Babe, I love you but you are thirty-three. We have careers as college professors. I think that the chances of you making it as a professional cage fighter have passed you by."

The bell rung. Gina glared at her husband, put her mouth piece in, and walked back out to the center of the cage. She was tired and her hands were low at her sides. She stared circling to her opponent's right when saw a sudden movement to her left. Gina saw another bright flash of purple and white.

Gina slowly opened her eyes to see a bright white light above her. She heard a muffled sound like a roar. She squinted her eyes several times and multiple shapes started to come into focus which slowly started to take the form of several men. She blinked again and the face of one of the men above her morphed into her husband.

Henry was yelling at her, "Gina, can your hear me?"

She slowly nodded and the slight motion sent a wave of pain rolling through her head.

Gina's head lolled to the left and she saw the referee holding up her opponent's hand in victory. The woman climbed on top of the cage and made a gesture to the crowd which indicated that she should be a champion of some kind. She then leapt off the cage and walked toward Gina. Gina could see that the woman was coming over to shake hands in a sign of good sportsmanship. Gina tried to sit up, but as soon as she made the attempt, she immediately slumped back onto the mat.

Henry scooped her up in his arms. "We are getting you to a hospital now!" He carried her out of the arena and to the car they had rented. He gently placed her down in the back of the car and said, "Stay awake! You may have a concussion!"

Gina groaned in reply and then she curled her legs up as Henry sped out of the parking lot. When the car started to move, another wave of pain shot through her head and she groaned both in pain and frustration. She would never admit it to him but Henry was right. What in the hell was she doing fighting in a semi-pro MMA event? She thought back about how she had arrived at this point.

Based on the writings of a few sailors who claimed to have seen canoes off the coast of Antarctica, she had convinced the board of trustee's at Princeton University to let her lead an expedition to the frozen continent in search of a lost tribe. She told the board that proving the existence of the lost tribe would be the anthropological find of the twenty-first century.

After a lot of debating, and with a good deal of trepidation, the board finally agreed to let Gina and her husband lead an expedition to Antarctica. She understood that her reputation and possible her job were riding on this expedition. She had seen pictures from that the sailors had taken, and by the formation of the canoe and the style of clothing that the people were wearing, she was sure that the tribe existed.

Still, several months of searching for a lost tribe, she had turned up nothing. For several years, Gina had utilized MMA training in order to exercise and relieve stress. As the stress of a failed expedition started to wear on her, Gina increased her training. When she was unable to gain any new leads on the lost tribe, her frustration reached the point that she decided to try engaging in her first official match. As another wave of pain tore through her head and her temple started to throb like a jack rabbit's heart, she regretted her brash decision to enter the cage. She was a woman in her thirties with multiple advanced degrees and now she was faced with the possibility of spending what little time that her expedition had left sitting in dark hotel room and nursing a concussion.

The car pulled to an abrupt stop in front of the hospital. Henry flung the door open which sent of wall of light pouring into the car. Gina rolled away from the glaring lights causing Henry to have to reach even farther into the car to pull her out. She did not feel as unsteady as she did back at the gym and she was able to walk into the hospital with little help from Henry. She turned to her husband. "Look, I was stupid to get into the cage and my head hurts but I think that I am okay. Can we please just go back to the hotel where I can lay down?"

Henry shook his head. "There is no way that I am letting you fall asleep until I know that you don't have a concussion. You know that if you go to sleep with a concussion that you could wake up dead." He smiled at his little joke as he eased her down into a chair in the crowded emergency room.

Gina looked around her at a room full of people who were suffering from all sorts of ailments. Clearly there was some form of gastritis or dysentery going around from the all of the people that were holding bags to vomit in. A good number of people were also coughing profusely and barely covering their mouths. Gina was not one of those people who was terrified of sick people, but she felt that staying in this hospital would do her health more harm than good. She stood up with ease as the effects of the blow to her head continued to subside. She was about to walk over to Henry when an old man wearing a seal skin outfit walked into the hospital carrying a girl who was severely wounded if not already dead. A frantic dock worker was walking behind the old man.

Several nurses ran over to the man. One of them grabbed the girl and rushed her into an operating room. The nurses were asking the old man several questions in Spanish but it was clear that he did not speak the language. Gina watched as the old man turned to the nurse and tried to communicate with her. To Gina's astonishment, she heard the language of the ancient Incas being spoken by the man. The nurses turned to frantic dock worker who addressed them in Spanish. "He just rowed up to the dock in a canoe. I couldn't understand what he was saying but as soon as I saw how badly the girl was hurt I immediately drove them here." Several of the nurses moved the dock worker over the check-in table as the old man continued to try and address the nurses in ancient Incan.

Henry's head turned to Gina. The two of them were likely the only two people in the hospital who spoke the man's language. They were both also thinking that based on the man's clothes and language that he might be a member of the tribe that they were looking for.

Gina ran over and she quickly asked the man in his own language what happened to his daughter. The man replied, "We have been traveling here for nearly three days by canoe from my homeland on the ice. She was taken by the Yeti and when he returned her to us she was badly injured. Please tell these people to save her life!"

Gina nodded and then she began speaking to the nurse, "He has traveled here from Antarctica. His has been traveling for nearly three days. He says that his daughter was attacked by…" Gina stopped for a moment when she realized that the man had said Yeti. In ancient Incan, the term is more like *giant wild man* but his intention was clear. In order to get the young girl help as quickly as possible, she rephrased the man's statement, "By a large animal."

The nurse nodded. "With a puncture wound that large and that deep, it must have been a walrus. It is their mating season. If she stumbled across a beach master looking for a female in heat, it may have attacked her."

The nurse turned and ran back to give the information to the doctors. Gina introduced herself and Henry to the old man. Gina helped the old man over to a seat away from all of the people who were coughing and vomiting. Gina's body was flush with adrenaline and the effects of her recent knockout had totally subsided. She spoke to Henry in English, "Quick, get him something to eat and drink. He looks nearly dehydrated."

Henry ran off and Gina talked softly to the old man in ancient Incan,."My name is Gina Murella and that is my husband Henry Murella. He will get you some food and something to drink." She placed her hand on the old man's shoulder. "What is your name?"

The old-man kept his eyes focused on the doors that led to the operating room. "Jun-Tuk."

Gina smiled. "Look, I want to make sure that your daughter gets as much help as possible. Did you say that a Yeti took your daughter and returned her with that injury?"

Jun-Tuk nodded. "I did. It was a large and powerful Yeti. My daughter offered herself to the Yeti in order that he would protect our village from the demons that live in the valley which is sounded by the mountains of ice." He took a deep breath. "She put her life in danger to protect my people and they would not risk letting the outside world find out about us in order to try and save her."

Gina cursed herself for not having a recorder or at least a notebook handy to take down the details of Jun-Tuk's story. Gina was anxious to try and get more information from the old-man, but despite her enthusiasm she knew that now was not the time to interrogate Jun-Tuk. Jun-Tuk was exhausted, and most importantly concerned with whether his daughter would live or die. Gina forced herself to stop being an anthropologist and to be start being a human. She placed her hand on his shoulder and addressed Jun-Tuk in his own language. "If there is anything that you need or that you need me to tell the doctors, just let me know."

Jun-Tuk nodded and smiled at Gina. Henry came rushing over with a bottled water and a sandwich that he had gotten from the hospital café. Jun-Tuk drank the water but he only took a few small bites from his sandwich. Hours passed as they waited for news from the doctors about Shunu's condition. The first rays of dawn had just pierced through the hospital windows when a doctor came out into the waiting room. He walked straight over to Jun-Tuk and Gina.

The doctor looked at Gina. "My nurses tell me that you are able to translate for this man."

Gina nodded. "Yes doctor."

The doctor knelt down beside Jun-Tuk. "I am sorry to have to tell you this but your daughter has died."

Gina's eyes began to tear up as she tried to form the words to tell Jun-Tuk but he could tell from the look on her face what had happened. The old man screamed, then he fell to the floor in a ball, and cried. Jun-Tuk began screaming even though Gina and Henry were the only people who could understand him. "They could have saved her! Had they only helped us reach the continent or halted the Yeti's abductions, they could have saved her! Were it not for their superstitions, Shunu would still be alive!"

Gina sat down on the floor next to Jun-Tuk and she cradled him in her arms. Gina barely knew this man but she could only guess at the anguish that he was in. It took a few minutes, but Gina and Henry were finally able to walk Jun-Tuk outside of the hospital. The old man stumbled into a dark corner where he sobbed for nearly a half an hour before he finally walked back over to Gina and Henry. "You speak my language. That means that you are educated. No doubt you are leaders of your people and instruct them with your knowledge."

Gina took a step closer to him. "Yes, that is exactly what we do. We teach people and we seek to gain new knowledge. Like knowledge about you and your people."

Jun-Tuk looked off in the direction of the ocean. "For too long, my people have forsaken knowledge in favor of fear and superstition. They have let the Yeti and the demons of the valley rule our lives. This fear has cost my daughter her life and many other young girls their lives as well." He placed his hand on Gina's shoulder. "You are a teacher who seeks to gain understanding of my people and their ways. I am a person who sees that my people need to be taught in the ways of the modern world in order to move past their fears. I think that we can both help each other. I will take you to my people so that you may study them, but in order for them to allow you access to the tribe you must first prove that the Yeti is nothing more than a beast. That he and the creatures which inhabit the valley are not gods and demons but that they are simply animals." Jun-Tuk looked into Gina's eyes. "I warn you, Dr. Murella, that if you are to agree to attempt this expedition, it will place the lives and the lives of all of the others that you take with you in danger." The hunter took a deep breath. "After my daughter was taken from me, I did something forbidden. I did what no other man in tribe has done before me. I went into the valley of the Yeti. I was only in there in for a short time but when I was in the valley, I saw beasts of tremendous ferocity and power, but they were beasts not demons. That fact that they are not the spawn of the underworld does not make them any less dangerous. The animals in the valley are as deadly as the Yeti himself. With that knowledge in mind, would you still lead your people into the valley?"

Gina bit her bottom lip and she was silent for moment. She took a quick look at her husband and then she nodded. "We'll do it."

CHAPTER 2

After helping Jun-Tuk make the preparations to have his daughter cremated, Gina and Henry were back in their hotel room. Gina had just finished contacting everyone who had accompanied them to Argentina to let them know that they needed to prepare for one last trip to Antarctica in the morning. Most of the people were hoping to return home rather than engage in another fruitless trip to the frozen wasteland but Gina promised them that this trip would be a success.

When she finally hung up the phone, she found Henry staring at her. She sighed. "Don't start with me, Henry. Just don't start. This is the best lead that we have had since we got here."

Henry sat down on their bed. "Look, I will admit the fact that he speaks ancient Incan is promising, but isn't possible that he is just an Incan descendant who lives in some remote area?"

Gina shrugged. "There are no recorded pockets of Incan descendants in this area. Even if that's all that he is, at least that would be a find of some significance to justify our expedition here. Right now, we have nothing to show for it. Not to mention the fact that his clothing is similar to the accounts that we have from sailors who have sighted the lost tribe."

Henry shook his head. "His story sounds crazy though. I mean come on, a lost tribe is one thing, but an actual Yeti? I mean even if you want to take a big leap and believe that Yetis exist, wouldn't they be in Nepal?"

Gina smiled. "It's a difficult translation and Yeti is the closest word that we have. First of all, I doubt it's an actual Yeti. A much more likely explanation is that there is a less civilized tribe who dress in the skins of animals in order to get Jun-Tuk's tribe to give them young women of a breeding age. Throughout history, tribes of people have taken women from other groups of people in order to diversify their breeding populations. If that's true, how great would it be to find two lost tribes? The people back at Princeton would fund expeditions for the next decade if that was the case."

Henry's voice took on a serious tone. "Okay, let's say there is another lost tribe of vicious wild-men. Did you see the wound on that girl? It looked like a walrus ran her through with its tusks. If this supposed second tribe exists as well, are we really prepared to deal with encountering a hostile tribe? I mean traveling across Antarctica is dangerous enough without encountering a tribe of killers. Not to mention the fact that Jun-Tuk talked about other dangerous animals living there."

Gina grabbed her husband's hand. "Henry, we have hunting rifles and shotguns if things get really bad."

Henry backed away from his wife in surprise. "Killing a rogue polar bear or something is one thing, but what about your suggested hostile tribe? Are you saying that you are willing to kill another human being just to save our careers?"

Gina shook her head. "God no. I am sure that if this is a primitive tribe, simply firing a few shots into the ground will scare them off. If they have never seen firearms before then a simple example of what we can do will frighten them. Jun-Tuk himself has said that his people avoid the modern world out of fear of our technology. Surely a less advanced tribe would be even more scared of us than Jun-Tuk's people." She wrapped her arms around her husband. "Henry, this is the break that we have been looking for. It's probably the last chance on Earth to study a culture that has evolved completely on its own without interaction with other civilizations. We'll be fine. There is nothing that we are going to run into down there that we are not prepared for. We have a team of over forty people including grad students, guides, mountaineers, and don't forget we have those hunters, Gordon and Rodgers. Even if there is a giant Yeti down there, they can more than handle it."

Henry nodded as he considered all of Gina's reasons for taking a chance on this last trip to Antarctica. Gina pushed him back onto the bed as she delivered the final reason for him to accept the expedition. "Besides, it's really cold down there and I am going to need someone to keep me warm."

The next morning, Gina was standing on the docks as she was taking inventory of the supplies that were being loaded onto the ship by her team. They had insulated tents, extra coats, thermal pants, goggles, face masks, insulated sleeping bags and portable heaters to deal with the cold. Gina checked off several snowmobiles, several large Sno-Cats, and even two teams of dog sleds in case of an emergency where their technology did not work. They also had four mobile barracks. One of the barracks served as a mobile lab. It was equipped with all of the materials that they would need to carry out an anthropological study. The lab barracks also contained the team's polar expedition gear, such as tents and heavy coats. The last part of the barracks contained an area where the hunters stored their weapons. The second barracks was split into two halves. The first half contained a small kitchen that stored the team's food. The other half of the second barracks contained several showers and restrooms. The final two barracks were set up to be sleeping quarters for the male and female team members. Each barracks would be towed to the campsite by one of the Sno-Cats.

Next, Gina moved onto the food. They had plenty of canned food and bottled water to use during their journey. If worst came to worst, they had enough supplies to the last them for five weeks until a rescue team arrived.

Once Gina was sure that they had everything they would need to make the journey, she started reviewing the materials that she needed to document whatever they found. She inventoried sample bags, cameras, notebooks, tablets, flares, and excavation materials just in case they needed to dig something out of the snow. She took special care to note that the dynamite they had for excavation was properly stored in order to ensure that it would not accidentally explode.

She did not directly check the specialist materials herself. She let the specialists in each field make their own inventory and then had them review it with her. The two hunters, Tony Gordon and Sam Rogers, were the first team of specialists to approach her. Tony Gordon was a tall, well-built man in his mid-twenties. He reviewed about a dozen shotguns and rifles that he was bringing aboard. Gina, Henry, and a few others had been given basic training and practice with these weapons. He also had a series of handguns that only he and Rodgers were cleared to utilize.

Sam Rodgers was much older than Gordon. He was in his fifties, balding, and he had a bit of a beer gut starting to form over what was once a well-conditioned body. While Gordon handled the firearms, Rodgers handled the other weapons. Rodgers had been on several hunting expeditions to the North Pole and Alaska. He had contended that on more than one occasion, he had seen firearms freeze up under sub-zero conditions. He insisted that he bring several crossbows and large hunting knives with him that he could count on. Only Rodgers, Gina, and Gordon were cleared to utilize the crossbows.

While Rodgers was an expert in his field, he was also the type of person who thought that he should be in charge of every situation that the team encountered. On several occasions, Gina and Rodgers had arguments over how the team should proceed when faced with an obstacle. Gina did not appreciate Rodgers questioning her authority in front of the rest of team and she made that clear to him at the expense of the hunter's pride. While Rodgers did not like taking orders from anyone, Gina felt that he was particularly frustrated that he was taking orders from a woman. After several of their arguments, Gina heard Rodgers walking way and muttering things like, "Stupid broad." Or "Probably her time of the month."

While Gina did not care for Rodgers personally, she could not argue with his capabilities in the field. Gina and Henry had hypothesized that if there was a lost tribe in Antarctica, they would most likely rely on seals for food, fuel, and clothing. Seals were the only large animals that humans could hunt that would supply them with the resources they would require to meet their basic needs for survival. Based on this idea, Gina had decided to follow local seal populations in hopes that they would lead the team to the lost tribe. At first, the team was only able to locate beaches where the seals had landed but not the seals themselves. Still from the evidence that the seals had left behind, Rodgers had been able to determine the size of each seal group and the direction that the seals had traveled after they had left the beach.

Gina had decided to only follow seal groups that were large enough to sustain a tribe that had a population of at least five hundred people. Rodgers had been able to locate each seal group that Gina had suggested to follow. So far none of the seal groups had led them to any evidence of a lost tribe but that was not Rodgers' fault. He had found the seals with little trouble. So while Gina was disgusted by Rodgers, she tolerated him because he was extremely efficient at his job.

After she had finished reviewing the hunters' supplies with them, her next task was to check on the medical supplies. Dana Summers was the ship's doctor. Like Gina, Dana was in her mid-thirties and tall with an athletic build. Outside of Henry, Dana was the only other person on the ship that Gina looked at as a friend. There were other young women on board the ship, but they were all there in the capacity of graduate students. Those women were Gina's responsibility. They were not her friends. Unlike the students, Dana was Gina's professional equal and as the ship's doctor, she also bore numerous responsibilities. Being on equal footing allowed the two women to converse with and confide in each other. Gina truly felt that Dana's friendship was one of the things that helped her to maintain her sanity during their expeditions.

Aside from being a good friend, Dana was also an excellent doctor. She was fully prepared for any emergency that could arise during their trip to Antarctica. Dana had supplies for everything from stomach viruses and the flu to injuries that could occur out on the ice. Dana also had numerous methods stored to deal with the threats posed by frostbite on a trip into sub-zero temperatures. In a worst case scenario, Dana had the necessary materials to amputate a finger or toe that had suffered such a severe case of frostbite that it needed to be removed in order to prevent infection to the rest of the body.

Gina boarded the ship and went to the medical bay to complete the final check of the medical supplies with Dana. The university required Gina to send a complete list of medical supplies to them before they would wire the money to ship's captain in order for him to set sail. Gina opened the door to the medical bay to see Gordon standing shirtless in front of Dana. Gordon turned around and gave a Gina a good look at his huge biceps, bulging pectoral muscles, and six-pack abs.

Gina quickly turned around and apologized, "I'm sorry. I should have knocked before I entered."

Gordon replied in his usual calm tone, "No apology necessary, Doctor Murella. I was just finishing up with my mandatory physical." He turned back toward Dana. "Is there anything else that you need from me, Doctor Summers?"

Dana shook her head. "No, as usual you are the picture of perfect health, Mister Gordon."

Gordon started putting his shirt back on. "Thanks, Doctor Summers." The young hunter turned to leave the room. He nodded at Gina as he walked by her. "Have a good day, Doctor Murella."

Gina smiled at the well-built hunter. "You too, Gordon." When the hunter had left the room, Gina quickly refocused on her purpose for coming to the medical bay. "Okay Dana, I know that you have everything ready to go. So just run over the medical checklist so that I can send a copy back to Princeton to prove to them that everything is on order." Dana walked over to Gina and then led her around the medical bay as the two women checked off everything on Princeton's mandatory medical supply list.

After Dana had finished reviewing her supply list with Gina, the young doctor turned to her friend. "This is both our best shot and our last shot at finding a lost tribe, isn't it?"

Gina nodded. "That is a yes on both accounts. Princeton won't continue to fund us if we don't come up with hard evidence of the lost tribe on this trip to Antarctica." Gina's voice softened slightly as she switched from her role as Dana's team leader to the role of her friend. "It also means that it's the best and last chance you will have to make a move on a certain strong and silent young hunter."

Dana's face quickly turned red. "You know that just because I said that Gordon was hot doesn't mean I want to date him or anything. I just happened to think that he is attractive."

Gina smiled at her friend and shrugged. "I am just saying, you don't want to look back at this trip and regret what might have been if you had made a move. Besides, on top of being hot, he seems like a pretty good guy." Gina turned and walked away. "You are not afraid to go on a trip across the world to one of coldest and deadliest place on Earth. You can perform emergency surgery on a glacier without blinking an eye, but when it comes to making a move on a guy you don't have the guts to do it?"

Gina turned and left the room. "One more thing to think about, you know that if I had never asked Henry out we would both probably still be single at this time. Sometimes, you just have to woman up and go after what you want." Gina left the room as Dana stood looking at her friend with a smile on her face.

With everyone and everything else on board the ship for the expedition, the only remaining person that Gina needed was Jun-Tuk himself. Early in the morning, Gina had arranged for a taxi to pick up Jun-Tuk and first to take him to the city morgue where he could pick up his daughter's ashes. Once Jun-Tuk had his daughter's ashes, the taxi was to bring him to the ship. Gina figured that the trip should have taken about an hour. She looked down at her watch to see that it had now been two-and-a-half hours since the taxi had picked up Jun-Tuk. Gina sighed and then reminded herself that while this trip was a career move for her, for Jun-Tuk it was a trip where he would be taking his daughter to her final resting place. At the same time, he was also trying to change the entire spiritual beliefs of his people. Once Gina had considered how difficult both of those tasks would be for anyone, she decided that she could be patient with Jun-Tuk if he needed extra time to prepare himself for this journey.

Gina felt that her time could best be served by getting in some exercise and relieving some of the stress that was building up inside of her. She sat down on the floor and began stretching. After she had completed her stretches, Gina stood up and began running laps around the ship. She had ran for roughly twenty minutes when she saw a taxi pull up to the dock. Jun-Tuk emerged from the taxi with the urn cradled in his arms.

As Jun-Tuk walked up the long ramp to the ship, he kept his eyes fixed on the urn. When he boarded the ship, he turned to Gina. "Please show me where I will be staying during our journey across the sea." Gina nodded then she led him to his cabin. When Jun-Tuk entered the cabin, he looked around at his temporary and signed. Then he placed his daughter's urn on the small table next to his bed. He then turned to Gina. "Have the ship go in a south west direction. When we reach the Antarctic coast, continue to have the ship head west." He turned to the remains of his daughter on the table next to him. "I should like to remain alone until we reach the coast. When it is in sight, please come and alert me. From there, I shall direct you as to where to land the ship."

Gina nodded and then she exited the room and closed the door. As she walked toward the bridge to give the captain his directions, her mind wondered if Jun-Tuk was truly in the right state of mind to lead an expedition across the Antarctic. She also wondered if she was in her right mind for placing the grieving father in the position that he was currently in.

CHAPTER 3

After sailing for nearly six hours, the ship had reached the coast of Antarctica. While Gina was anxious to talk to Jun-Tuk about his tribe, she had respected the man's wish for solitude during their journey. When the coast was within sight, Gina went to Jun-Tuk's cabin, knocked on the door, and called out to him. Jun-Tuk answered the door. He was still dressed in the same clothes that he had worn when made the journey across the ocean in a canoe. The old man had a distinct smell to him at this time. Gina was used to interacting with people who lived in primitive settings and who had limited access to bathing and methods through which to wash their clothes. Gina took shallow breaths and she made sure that her facial expressions did not offend the old man.

Jun-Tuk did not say anything; he simply waited for Gina to lead him to the front of the ship and he silently followed her. As they approached the front of the ship, they noticed that nearly the entire team was gathered at the front of the vessel. They were all staring at a group of seals that was frantically moving in and out of the surf. Gina and Jun-Tuk walked over to join the group and see what was causing the seals to be so upset.

When they had reached the side of the ship, Gina saw why the seals were behaving in a panicked manner. Her eyes shifted to the ocean where she saw to large bulges of water streaking toward the beach like giant torpedoes. She watched in awe as two orcas rode the surf into the beach itself. The massive animals crashed onto the beach and into the midst of the terrified seals. Each of the orcas snapped its jaws closed on a fleeing seal. The orcas then rolled their bodies back into the water until they were deep enough to swim back out to sea.

The orcas took the injured animals out to deep water where they tossed their prey high into the air and let them crash into the ocean before devouring them. As the two successful orcas played with their food, another set of the creatures rode the waves into the gathered seals.

Gina and Jun-Tuk stood next to Rodgers as the hunter looked at the orcas with obvious admiration. "Those orcas are true apex predators. There is nothing in the Antarctic that can rival their hunting prowess." He looked toward Jun-Tuk. "Isn't that right, my friend? No other predator in these parts rivals the orca?"

Gina translated for Jun –Tuk who replied in his native language. "Nothing in the sea. On land, the Yeti has no equal."

Gina smiled and looked at Rodgers, "He says that you are right." Gina had yet to talk to her team about the Yeti. She knew that after several failed trips to find a lost tribe that throwing in a tall tale about a Yeti would make them even more skeptical about their chances of success. With the thought of the expedition at the forefront of her mind, she tried to press Jun-Tuk about where they would go ashore. "Jun-Tuk where are we taking the ship from here?"

The old man pointed to the west. "Continue along the shoreline in the direction of the sun until the sun sets, the moon completes his journey across the sky, and the sun rises once more. When we reach that point, we will see the mountains. From there, you will go ashore and find the pass that leads into the valley of the Yeti."

Gina looked at Jun-Tuk with a confused look on her face, "Jun-Tuk, I thought that we were going to meet your tribe first. Once I gain their confidence then I can show them that the Yeti is nothing more than a superstition."

Jun –Tuk's face remained stoic. "I can assure you that unless you bring proof that the Yeti is not a divine creature with you, the people of my tribe will kill you and all of the others in your group. I can also assure you that while the Yeti is not a god, it is far more than a superstition." He turned away from Gina. "It was more than a simply superstition that took my daughter from me." Jun-Tuk then walked slowly back to his cabin.

Gina cursed herself for once more not being sensitive to the fact that the man was still in a deep state of grief. She had hoped to avoid the Yeti discussion with her team until they had successfully studied and documented Jun-Tuk's tribe. She took a deep breath and decided that she had better get her team together and advise them of the course of action that they would be taking in the next twenty four hours. She yelled at the gathered people watching the orcas, "Alright everyone, please gather in the galley. We have to discuss the next aspect of our expedition."

Gina quickly grabbed Henry and pulled him into their room prior to addressing the other members of the team. "Jun-Tuk is insisting that we need to gather proof that the Yeti is only an animal before he shows us where his tribe is located. He says that unless we show up in the village with proof in hand, they will chase us away from their village if not outright kill us."

Henry shrugged. "Okay so how are you going to approach this with the team?"

Gina sighed. "I am just going to explain to them that this supposed Yeti is probably nothing more than another lost tribe. I will emphasize that this tribe is probably using the superstitious beliefs of Jun-Tuk's tribe in order to acquire young females to expand their breeding population."

Henry gave her a sarcastic smile. "Okay, if you think that explaining the situation to them that way will convince them to go on a Yeti hunt."

Gina placed her hand on her hip and glared at her husband. "Do you have a better idea?"

Henry shook his head. "No. I can't think of a better way to explain to people that we are going on a Yeti hunt."

Gina let out a dramatic sigh. "First of all, stop calling it a Yeti hunt. This is an opportunity to study two undocumented tribes rather than one. That's how we are going to explain this to everyone."

Gina started to walk out of the room when Henry grabbed her. "Look, we don't know what's out there. We can't just tell everyone that we are looking for a second tribe when we don't know for sure what's taking those girls."

Gina gave her husband a curious look. "You are not saying that I should go down there and tell those people that we are going after an actual Yeti are you?"

Henry shrugged again. "I am saying that you should tell them what Jun-Tuk has told us. I am saying that you tell them your thoughts on the situation, and then you let them make their own conclusions about what we are facing. Then let them decide if this trip is something that they want to be a part of or not. What we can't do is not give these people all of the information that we have if there is even the slightest chance that we might be walking into a dangerous situation. Yeti, aggressive tribe, or Godzilla, if there is any chance of us walking into a dangerous situation, those people need to know about it."

The anger flowed out of Gina's body and she smiled at her husband. "You're right. I will fill them in on everything that we know about the situation." She hugged her husband. "Thank you, as always you are my voice of reason."

Henry hugged her back. "And you are the passionate risk taker who pushes me to get all I can out of life. We balance each other out pretty well."

The two of them then let go of each other and walked down to the galley. When they entered the room, Gina was not surprised to see Rodgers and Gordon sitting near the front of the group. Gordon no doubt wanted to be as informed as possible which just further justified Henry's point and Rodgers would be looking for any opportunity that he could to take control of the meeting.

Gina calmed herself downed and addressed the people who were literally following her to the ends of the earth. "Okay everyone, as you know, we are following the lead of a native of the tribe that we are looking for. He had a caveat to his agreement to take us to his tribe."

She took a deep breath. "Now before I tell you what he wants us to do, I want you to remember that we are dealing with a tribe that has had limited exposure to the outside world and modern technology. Their culture is still very much steeped in mysticism and superstition. According to Jun-Tuk, his village has long been visited by a Yeti that will occasionally take the young women from his tribe."

Everyone in the crowd either laughed or started talking amongst themselves. Gina immediately tried to maintain control of the meeting. "Look everyone, I think we can rest easy and assume that we are not dealing with an actual Yeti. What we are probably dealing with is a another missing tribe that is using what are likely to be elaborate costumes to scare Jun-Tuk's tribe into giving them women of a breeding age. Jun-Tuk reports that sometimes the woman comes back after the Yeti has taken them. I have questioned Jun-Tuk about this and I specifically asked him if any of the women who returned were pregnant. He assured me that none of them were, which would lead to the logical conclusion that the women who did not return were indeed impregnated by this other tribe."

Gina took a moment to catch her breath as the crowd quieted down. "Jun-Tuk does not believe that the Yeti is a spirit. He says that in order for his tribe to allow us access to study them, we need to bring back proof that the Yeti is not an all-powerful god."

A hand went up in the crowd. "How exactly are we going to do that if we believe that the Yeti is actually the members of another perhaps hostile tribe?"

Gina shook her head. "This is the main reason that I am addressing this situation with you. I hope that we can simply take pictures of this tribe and the skins that they use as costumes. After we study the tribe from afar, we can consider if it is worth approaching them and offering to trade them for proof that they are the Yeti. Then we can go back to Jun-Tuk's tribe and have access to study them as well." She took a sip of water. "Now, while we were not expecting to undertake this extra expedition, it does present us with an excellent opportunity to study not just one lost tribe but two. That being said, given how this other tribe seems to operate, it may be more dangerous than we had originally thought. If anyone would like to back out now, I am offering to pay for your services up until this point and to give you full credit for your work." Gina looked over the crowd. "Is there anyone who would like to back out?" The entire team was silent. Gina smiled. "Good, it's settled then. We will proceed with a two-part expedition. Are there any other questions?"

Gina was not surprised to see Rodgers raise his hand. "Have we considered the fact that what Jun-Tuk is saying is true? That there really is a Yeti out there? Before you scoff at me, I would like to point out that Native African reports of gorillas in the jungle were scoffed at by European explorers until a white man saw them. Should we not consider that this could be the case here and prepare accordingly?"

Gina glared at Rodgers. "In the interest of the safety of the people on board, you and Gordon can prepare as if there may be a large animal out there. I am going to emphasize though that this is not some kind of History Channel monster hunt. If we find a second tribe that looks like it is perpetrating this Yeti legend then we are studying the tribe, not hunting for a monster."

Rodgers nodded. "That sounds reasonable enough but if there is a Yeti then how are you going to proceed?"

Gina's blood began to boil at Rodgers' arrogance. She replied with a sharp tone in her voice, "If there is a Yeti then I will decide how we proceed from there. Now are there any other questions?" Gina looked over the silent room. "Good then start preparing. We will be going ashore in a few hours."

Gina walked out of the room with Henry behind her. Henry whispered into her ear, "You had better hope that there is no Yeti or Rodgers will never let you hear the end of it."

She grumbled, "Believe me, I know."

CHAPTER 4

Gina climbed down into the small motor boat that was going to take the team from the ship to the shore. Even through her insulated boots, she could feel how cold the water was below the small vessel. She had made the trip to land on a small motor boat like this before, but as she looked over at Jun-Tuk sitting calmly next to her, she gained a new-found respect for the old man who had made the trip across this freezing water in nothing more than a seal skin canoe.

Once Henry, Rodgers, Gordon, and Dana Summers were onboard, the motor boat began to speed toward the frozen shores of Antarctica. The serene white landscape of the continent still awed Gina. To most people, Antarctica was a barren wasteland, but to Gina it was a pristine landscape and the last large area of land that had yet to be conquered and overrun by man. The transport boat had to be careful when it tried to go ashore because of the rocky ocean bottom that comprised most of the Antarctic coast. There were only a few very spread out sandy beaches that the transport boats could land on.

When the boat reached the shore, and Gina stepped back onto Antarctica, she almost felt as if she was home. Gina scanned the horizon and in the distance, she could see the mountain range that Jun-Tuk had spoken of. A thrill of excitement ran through Gina's spine. In a few short hours, she would be the first person to see and document a tribe which had never been seen by a person born outside of Antarctica.

She looked back over her shoulder as the boat that had dropped her off turned and headed back to ship. It would take five more trips to and from the ship to unload the expedition members and small equipment. A larger motor boat would make several trips to bring the vehicles to shore.

Nearly three hours after Gina had first stepped ashore, the last of the large vehicles was finally unloaded from the larger motor boat. The team immediately went to work loading up the Sno-Cats.

Gina climbed to the top of the lead Sno-Cat with her binoculars in hand. She called for Jun-Tuk to join her. Gina reached her hand down to help the old man up onto the Sno-Cat, when to Gina's surprise, he climbed to the top of the machine even quicker than she had. She reminded herself that despite his age, the old man had singlehandedly rowed a canoe from here to South America. Gina took a look through her binoculars at a mountain range that for the most part until now had gone undocumented. There had been satellites which had caught the mountains on camera previously, but because of their remote location, no one had ever explored the polar mountain range. From where Gina was standing, it almost looked like two separate mountain ranges ran perpendicular to each other and came to a point at a sharp right angle. One mountain range seemed to run from east to west as far as she could see. The second mountain range ran north and south. This end of this mountains was also well out of the range of Gina's binoculars to follow. At the point where the two ranges came together, Gina could see a small upward hill that led in between the two mountains at the tips of the respective ranges.

She looked over at Jun-Tuk and smiled. "I would guess that we can reach the path that leads into the valley in just under two hours. The question from there is, how do we find this Yeti of yours?"

Jun-Tuk turned and looked into Gina's eyes with an icy cold stare. "The Yeti is a beast but it is a beast very much like a human. If there are humans nearby, the Yeti will sense us and he will come." He placed his hand on Gina's shoulder. "Shunu was injured badly. I do not know if the Yeti attained what he was looking to from his interaction with her. He will not come to the village if a woman dies, but with us being near him, he may decide to take one of the women from your team with him."

While Gina understood the threat posed by a potentially hostile tribe, she was also confident that her team could scare off a group of people who were still ruled by superstitions. She smiled. "Don't worry, Jun-Tuk, we will be prepared for the Yeti if he shows up."

Jun-Tuk shook his head. "Nothing can prepare you for the Yeti." The old man turned and climbed down off the Sno-Cat. Gina shrugged and called out to her team, "All right everyone load up! We are heading for the mountain range directly south of our current position!"

The trip went by quickly, and a little under a half an hour later, the expedition team had reached the mountain range. The mountain rang itself was huge; it could easily go on for hundreds of miles. The valley inside of the mountain range could easily have been as large as the area between the Rocky Mountains and the Pacific Ocean in North America. Gina reassured herself that the tribe they were looking for would have to be near the pass that Jun-Tuk was taking them to or else they would not be able to make the trips that they regularly did to Jun-Tuk's tribe. Gina had the team set up camp a half a mile from the entrance to the valley pass. She feared that the tribe she expected to find would be terrified if they saw the Sno-Cats and she wanted to study them in as natural a state as possible. This meant that she would need to keep the presence of her team hidden from the tribe as long as possible. She looked over the data that was streaming through the tablet in her Sno-Cat. A winter storm was heading directly for their current location. Snow had already begun to fall outside and it was covering the Sno-cats.

Most of her team members were busy setting up the camp but she wanted to take a quick look inside of the valley. She quickly gathered Henry, Jun-Tuk, Dana, Rodgers, and Gordon and told them that they would be taking a quick trip to scout the entrance to the pass ahead of the storm. They had about three hours until the storm hit. She figured that the hike to the entrance would take about a half hour. They had enough time to get an idea of what the valley looked like and document the area for an hour. They would then make the half hour hike back with an hour to spare ahead of the storm.

When her small team was fully prepped, they started hiking out to the valley pass with Jun-Tuk leading the way. Gordon and Rodgers both carried shotguns and Rodgers also kept his crossbow slung over his shoulder. The snow was starting to increase in volume and Gina began to wonder if the storm had not picked up speed. She kept a close eye on her watch and she was concerned when it took them nearly forty-five minutes to reach the pass.

When they reached the pass, Gina made some mental notes on the pass itself. The pass was in actuality a small path that ran between the bases of two separate mountains. The pass itself was roughly forty-feet wide and had a slight upward sloped to it that ended at the entrance to the valley. The incline was dotted with large boulders that Gina surmised must have rolled down off the mountains over the centuries. Gina scaled the small incline to get a look at the valley but all that she could see was the falling snow. It was like staring out into a blizzard. The others were standing beside her and she could already hear Rodgers mumbling about a wasted trip. Gina was about to start shouting at him when a loud noise echoed over the landscape.

Everyone except Jun-Tuk had a surprised look on their faces. Henry looked at Gina. "What the heck was that? It didn't come from camp. Whatever that was, it came from within the valley."

The sound repeated again and Rodgers walked up between Gina and Gordon. "I have been on numerous safaris and if I didn't know that we were near the South Pole, I would swear that was an elephant. What would you say, Gordon?"

The stoic hunter nodded. "It almost sounds like an elephant. The difference is that the trumpet sound that we just heard was louder and deeper than an elephant."

Jun-Tuk walked up beside Gina. "We need to conceal ourselves now!"

Gina yelled to everyone, "Quick! Take cover behind the rocks!"

Gina, Henry, and Dana all hid behind one of the large boulders and Rodgers, Gordon, and Jun-Tuk behind another. Gina could see a large brown form moving through the falling snow. She tried to focus her eyes on the object when another trumpeting sound echoed through the valley pass. A collective gasp went through Gina's team as a long, fur-covered trunk and two long, curved white tusks came into view. A massive shaggy head attached to a huge quadrupedal body came into view. Gina whispered to her husband and her best friend, "Please tell me that you see what I think I am seeing?"

Henry kept his eyes fixed on the creature. "If you think that you are seeing a wooly mammoth then yes."

Gina nodded. "Okay, I was almost hoping that I was going crazy. That thing has to be, what, at least twenty-five feet tall at the shoulder?" No one answered her as several more mammoths began to wander into their view through the falling snow.

Rodgers waved from behind the rock to get their attention. Once Gina was looking at him, he talked as loudly as he thought was safe, "They're migrating. That big one in the front is the alpha male. If he even thinks that we are a threat, they will charge us and these little pop guns won't do anything but piss them off. We just need to stay where we are until they pass by."

Gina nodded and then she continued to watch as an endless line of what was thought to be an extinct species continued to march by in front of them.

CHAPTER 5

Gina and Dana were sitting down having a warm cup of coffee. They had returned to the base camp and had informed everyone about what they had found inside of the valley. The obvious questions came up during their meeting with the staff: *If there are wooly mammoths in the valley, could there be other prehistoric animals? How should we proceed with documenting these creatures and studying them?* Both of those questions were valid. The mammoths and any other unusual creatures in the valley needed to be studied and documented. Therein was part of the problem. Gina's team was primarily composed of anthropologists. A situation like this required zoologists and paleontologists to properly study these animals. Those issues aside, the main question that came from the team members was: *If there are wooly mammoths in the valley, does that also mean that there is a Yeti in there as well?*

The meeting as a whole had to be cut short so the team members could properly prepare themselves and their equipment for the coming storm. As such, Gina put most of the questions on hold until she had time to consider the options in front of her regarding their next step. Gina and Dana were enjoying this last coffee before retiring to their quarters themselves. Dana was looking at Gina and she knew exactly what she was thinking. Dana also knew that she was the one person who could ask Gina difficult questions without aggravating her.

Dana put her coffee down. "So what are we going to do? Do we stay and study the animals in the valley or do we head back home and report our findings to Princeton so that they can send a more qualified team to study those animals."

Gina shook her head. "We know at least that the tribe Jun-Tuk is from is real and that it is here. We also know that they won't let us study them unless if we can prove that the Yeti is not a god." She took a deep breath. "We probably should head back to Princeton and report our findings. Going back to Princeton would be the safer and easier route to go. The problem with that is when the board weighs the find of woolly mammoths versus a lost tribe, they will put all of their resources into the valley. Our expedition will be dead in the water just as we had our first breakthrough in finding the lost tribe." Gina bit her lower lip in thought for a moment and then she looked at her friend. "We are going to study and document the mammoths and anything else that we find in the valley. We may not be specialized in animals or extinct species, but the basic concepts or studying them are the same as studying a lost tribe. We will document them the same way that we would Jun-Tuk's tribe. After we have enough information on the valley, and we can prove to Jun-Tuk's tribe that the Yeti is not a god, we will complete our study of them as well. When all is said and done, we can return to Princeton with our study fully complete as well as an initial study of the valley. That way we finish what we came here for, become famous for finding a lost tribe and this valley, and Princeton can send a more qualified team to follow up on the valley after us." Gina grinned. "If you have any interest, I am sure that the follow-up team will also need a team a doctor and an experienced young and handsome hunter."

Dana was about to say something when a horrible wailing sound came from outside. Dana gave Gina a concerned look. "What in the hell was that? It sure didn't sound like the mammoths did and it didn't sound like it came from within the valley. That sounded a hell of a lot closer."

The two women ran to the window of the barracks and they looked out into the dark blizzard that was taking place outside. At first, they couldn't see anything and then Gina gasped when she saw to bright red orbs floating in the air and moving toward the camp. Gina thought the eyes had a blood red hue to them. As the red orbs continued to move toward the camp, something else started to come into view as well. It was difficult to see because it was white just like the snow that was falling onto it, but as it took a few more steps forward, the gargantuan form of the Yeti came into view. Dana screamed when she saw the creature but Gina kept her eyes fixed on it taking mental notes on everything that she was seeing.

The creature was bipedal and covered in a thick white fur. The beast's ghastly face was accentuated by burning red eyes. The creature was very large. Gina guessed that it was between twenty and twenty-five feet tall, making it roughly as large as the mammoths that she had seen earlier. It had broad shoulders and slightly disproportionately long arms. The monster had primate like hands with a clearly opposable thumb. Its legs were thick and ended in feet that were also disproportionately large. Just by looking at it, Gina could see that the Yeti was extremely physically powerful. She could see its huge muscles shifting under its skin even with its thick white fur. The monster had a face that appeared almost human. It was dark and similar to a gorilla but with the visage of more intelligence than the great apes of Africa. The monster had long sharp fangs that protruded over both his upper and lower lips, and when he opened his mouth, Gina saw nothing but sharp teeth. She had no doubt that this beast was a carnivore and a predator. The last noteworthy feature was that the top of its head ended in a sharp dome.

As the Yeti entered the camp, it wailed again and started walking toward one of the barracks. As soon as Gina saw the Yeti making for the barracks, she sprang into action. She still had most of her outdoor gear on. All that she needed to do was to put on her coat, goggles, and boots. She flung the door open as she was getting dressed so that she could see what the Yeti was doing. When the door had opened fully, she could see the Yeti towering over one of the nearby barracks. The monster plunged his claw into the roof of the building and tore it off as it were made of cardboard. He tossed the roof aside and roared at the terrified people inside of it. Gina watched in horror as the Yeti reached into the opened barracks and lifted out a young man. The man was one of the interns. Gina recognized him as Eric Williams. The Yeti sniffed the man and then tossed him away. The young man screamed as he flew through the air then crashed into the snow.

Gina was fully dressed and about to run out at the Yeti when she saw Henry come sprinting out of one of the other barracks. He moved as quickly as he could through the thick snow to the nearest Sno-Cat. He climbed into the vehicle, turned its lights on, and spun it toward the Yeti. He then revved the machine up to full speed and aimed it at the beast. The Sno-Cat slammed into the Yeti as the monster was reaching into the opened barracks again. Gina was astounded that the Sno-Cat had collided with the Yeti and the two-ton vehicle did not move the creature an inch. She then watched in horror and disbelief as the Yeti lifted the several ton Sno-Cat, with Henry still in it, over its head. The Yeti roared and then threw the Sno-Cat nearly fifty feet from itself. The Sno-Cat landed upside down and Gina could see Henry squirming to get free from inside of the vehicle as the Yeti started walking toward it.

Gina moved faster than she ever would have thought possible. She grabbed two satellite radios, a transmitter, and a receiver from the supply closet. She tossed the receiver and one of the radios to Dana and then she sprinted out into the snow. As she was running, she turned on her radio and said, "Keep track of me but do not come for me unless I call for help. We can't lose any more lives!" Gina then turned off the radio and stuffed both it and the transmitter into her pockets.

Dana heard what her friend said over the radio but she didn't understand what she was talking about until she walked to the door and saw Gina running toward the Sno-Cat. The Yeti had almost reached the Sno-Cat, and her trapped husband, when Gina knelt down before the Yeti as had the young girl in Jun-Tuk's story. The Yeti stared at Gina for a moment and then he reached down and picked her up. The Yeti sniffed Gina, and when he did so, the beast seemed to calm down somewhat. The monster turned and began walking out of the camp with Gina held firmly in his claw.

From with the monster's grip, Gina could see Henry screaming in terror as the Yeti walked away with her. Gina held her gloved hands out in front of her and made the sign of a heart indicating to Henry that she loved him. She then looked up at the Yeti's beast-like face. Part of her wanted to scream in terror at the horrible fate that awaited her. Panic was setting in when she reminded herself of two things. First, that Jun-Tuk had said that the women who placated the Yeti were returned to their people unharmed. The second thing that she remembered was that she was a scientist. This thought more than anything else helped to calm her down and focus her. As a scientist, she owed it to the world to act in accordance with the standards of her profession. She was the first non-native to be taken by the Yeti and she needed to learn everything that she could about the creature and report back on her findings at the appropriate time. She was still terrified, but these thoughts helped her to focus on staying calm because she knew that staying calm would increase her chances of staying alive. She also knew that Henry was alive and that thought gave her comfort. Had Henry died, she would just have preferred that Yeti had devoured her as well. Henry was alive though and that thought gave Gina a reason to find a way to get back to him.

This thought had no sooner crossed her mind than she noticed that the Yeti was walking through the mountain pass and back into the valley. The blizzard was reaching its full intensity as they entered the valley. All that Gina could see around her was the blinding snow. She wondered to herself that if the valley held both mammoths and the Yeti what other "demons" as Jun-Tuk had called them also lived in the unexplored region?

Gordon and several of the other grad students ran over to the tossed Sno-Cat to try and help Henry. Henry was still screaming for his wife and trying desperately to free himself from the destroyed vehicle. Gordon kicked in the already-cracked windshield of the Sno-Cat and then he used his knife to cut Henry loose from his seatbelt.

Henry tumbled out through the open windshield and then he began running in the direction that the Yeti had taken Gina. Rodgers grabbed him and held him in place as he yelled into the panicked man's ear, "Henry, we will never catch that beast in this storm! Think! Several of the women have come back alive after being with the Yeti for over two weeks! There is every reason to believe that we will get her back alive, but if we head out into this storm unprepared to enter a valley that holds mammoths, a Yeti, and god knows what else, we will all die!"

Dana came running out into the snow with the radio and receiver. "She threw these too me before she gave herself to the Yeti in order to save Henry. We can track her and communicate with her." She was silent for a moment. "She specifically said though not to try and take her back from the Yeti unless she called for help. She said that we can't afford to lose any more lives."

Henry took a look around at the gathered people. "Tomorrow, I am going after my wife. Anyone who wants to accompany me is welcome to do so. Anyone who wants to stay back here at camp, you need to start packing up! As soon as I come back with Gina, we are going home!"

He turned to Rodgers. "Can you help me get the things together that we need to go into the valley with?"

Rodgers nodded. "Yes! Gordon and I will get started right away!" Most people returned to their barracks as Henry, Gordon, Rodgers, Dana and a handful of grad students started preparing for a journey into the unknown at first light.

CHAPTER 6

Between the storm, the darkness around her, and the speed at which the Yeti was moving, Gina had no idea how long she had been gone for or how far she had traveled. From the angle at which the Yeti was walking, Gina was fairly sure that the monster was walking on the side of one of the many mountains which comprised the mountain range which circled the valley. Gina's suspicion that they were walking on the side of the mountain was confirmed when the Yeti turned into a large cave and finally released her from his grip. The Yeti lumbered to the back of the cave where he laid down and quickly fell asleep. When she saw that the Yeti was asleep, Gina immediately thought about trying to escape from the monster but then the reality of her situation set in on her. There was a storm raging outside and she had no idea which direction she should travel in. She also did not have any of the gear required for a solo hike across an uncharted polar valley. She resolved herself to the fact that, for now, her best course of action was to stay with the Yeti. She checked her radio and her transmitter. She was relieved that both of communication devices were fully operational. Gina also reminded herself that the Yeti had returned most of the women that he had taken to their people after a two week period. Since the Yeti had left the valley to come to the camp, she was pretty sure that if she tried to escape, the Yeti would most likely find her. Gina remembered that Jun-Tuk believed that it was the women who placated the Yeti that returned alive. Gina spoke aloud to herself, "So if I am a perfect houseguest for the next two weeks, you will return me to my team and that will be then end of it. In that time, I can be the first person in history to study and document the life of a Yeti."

Gina resolve was solid but her body was freezing. It took her a moment to realize that the only source of heat in the cave was the Yeti himself. Gina had not really noticed it when they were walking through the snowstorm outside, but inside the confines of the cave, she quickly became aware of how horrible the Yeti smelled. Gina swallowed hard as she told herself that smelling bad was better than freezing to death. She pulled her scarf over her nose and mouth, walked over to the Yeti, and laid down beside him. Gina was exhausted and despite the circumstances that she was faced with, she quickly fell asleep.

Back in camp, Henry was trying to get the rescue party together as quickly as he could. He was yelling out random orders to people. Rodgers was cleaning guns and checking ammunition when Henry shouted at him, "Get the shotguns ready and onto the Sno-Cats! I want us tracking that beast within the hour!"

Rodgers stopped what he was doing and walked up to Henry. "Look, you need to sit down and shut up. You are not thinking clearly. Your wife has been taken by a monster and you want to save her. I can appreciate your desire to save her, but I will be dammed if I am going to let you put together a rushed expedition that gets us all killed. First of all, the shotguns will be useless. From what I have seen from the mammoths and the Yeti, anything less than a high-powered rifle is going to do us more harm than good. Did you even think about how rocky the pass to the valley is? There is no way in hell that the Sno-Cats will be able to make it over that terrain. The only way that we are going to get past those boulders is with the snowmobiles." Rodgers pointed to one of the remaining barracks. "Go sit down and get yourself ready to go into the valley. I will coordinate setting up the rescue team."

Henry was silent for a moment as he considered what Rodgers had said. Henry knew that Gina would loathe to give control of everything over to Rodgers, but he had to admit that Rodgers was right. Henry knew that he was not thinking straight because he was in such emotional distress over Gina's abduction. While he wanted to keep control over the expedition, more than anything else he wanted to get Gina back safely and Rodgers was his best bet at accomplishing that goal. He nodded. "Okay Rodgers, set things up and then come and get me when we are ready to head out into the valley."

Rodgers didn't reply. He simply nodded at Henry and then he started shouting out orders to the rescue team. Henry climbed down off the Sno-Cat and walked slowly back to the barracks with his mind thinking only of once again holding Gina safely in his arms again. He had no sooner closed the door to the barracks then

Jun-Tuk walked in behind him. The old man approached Henry and spoke in a very direct manner, "I have lost my daughter and I will not let you lose your wife. If you let the man who hunts for sport lead this rescue mission, your wife will be lost to you and many others will die. His concern is not for your wife. He is only concerned with his own glory. I know this area better than anyone else here. Please let me take you and your people into the valley. Let me help you save your wife and at the same time help to gather the proof to bring to my people that the Yeti is an animal and not a god."

Henry was silent for a moment. He knew that Rodgers would not take the news well that he was going to appoint Jun-Tuk the leader of the rescue mission, but he also didn't care. If Jun-Tuk was his best option at bringing his wife back alive then he would take that option. He stood up. "Let Rodgers finish directing the team on the preparations for the rescue mission and then I will tell him that you will be leading us once we enter the valley."

Jun-Tuk nodded then he turned and walked out of the barracks. The old man watched as the arrogant hunter continued to shout orders at the expedition members. Jun-Tuk shook his head in disgust. He knew that he was looking at the hunter who would either find his own death in the valley or bring death to all of those around him.

When Gina woke up, she found that the Yeti was still sleeping next to her. She took the time to study the Yeti in a somewhat more controlled setting than when she was first taken by the monster. As she looked at the Yeti, she realized that monster was even more terrifying than she had originally thought. The monster was clearly and apex predator and a killing machine. An up-close look at the monster's teeth and claws, quickly confirmed for her that the Yeti could kill a large steer with a single swipe of its hand. Gina was taking mental notes on the Yeti when she realized that she should give the creature a name as opposed to just referring to it by its species designation. After all, the Yeti had to be a member of a larger population. It was extremely unlikely that the monster was a King Kong-like last remaining member of species. Even if the Yetis were a solitary species, she figured that there was a decent chance that she would encounter other members of the species at some point. Gina had never really thought much about Yeti's. In fact, the only thing that Gina could even remember about Yeti's was the Bumble from the old Rudolph the Red-Nosed Reindeer claymation Christmas special that they show on television every year. She vaguely remembered there being a character named Yukon in the movie. As she looked at the Yeti, she nodded her head. "Yes, Yukon the Yeti, I even like the alliteration in the name."

A loud trumpeting sound that Gina immediately recognized as the sound of the mammoth herd echoed through the cave. As soon as the sound reached the cave, the Yeti's eyes snapped open and Yukon stood up. The cave that they were in was huge but when the Yeti stood up, his pointed head nearly touched the cave ceiling. The Yeti looked briefly at Gina then he approached the cave entrance and roared. After he had roared, Yukon went running down the slope of the mountain with at a speed that Gina could not believe the massive creature was capable of attaining. Gina may not have been a zoologist but she knew hunting behavior when she saw it. She sprinted to the entrance of the cave to observe how Yukon was going to prey on the mammoths.

At the sound of Yukon's roar, panic spread throughout the mammoth herd. The alpha male trumpeted loudly and Gina watched as the adult mammoths moved the infants to the inside of the herd. The alpha male then began running away from the mountain and the rest of the herd followed his lead quickly creating a stampede. There was a large bull mammoth toward the back of the herd that was not able to run as fast as the young mammoths, and when Yukon saw the beast fall behind, he changed direction and began running toward it. The mammoth was still trying to catch up with the rest of his herd when Yukon ran up alongside the animal and dug his claws into the mammoth's side. Bright red blood sprayed across the white snow as Yukon raked his claws across the mammoth's back. The mammoth bucked wildly and he was finally able to shake himself loose from Yukon's grip. The mammoth quickly spun around and faced Yukon. The mammoth pawed at the ground and trumpeted at the Yeti. The injured bull then lowered his head and charged at

Yukon. The mammoth moved faster than Yukon was prepared for and its huge curved tusks slammed into Yukon's chest and knocked the Yeti to the ground. Yukon was lying flat on his back as the mammoth quickly moved forward, bent his head down, and attempted to gore the Yeti. Gina watched as Yukon's hands shot up and caught the mammoth's tusks before they were able to reach his body.

Gina then watched in awe as, despite the weight and strength of the mammoth, Yukon was slowly forcing the mammoth to back up. Once he had gained some leverage, Yukon pushed the mammoth's tusks to the side, causing the beast's head to follow. Yukon sprang to his feet and moved in on the mammoth. When Yukon had reached the mammoth, the bull lowered its head then he used his long curved horns to hook under and around Yukon's shoulders while simultaneously wrapping its powerful trunk around Yukon's waist. Yukon responded by plunging his claws into the mammoth's neck. The two monsters wrestled as each creature tried to the throw the other to the ground. Once more in this test of strength it was Yukon who proved the stronger of the two beasts. Gina watched as Yukon was able to force the left side of the mammoth's legs to lift off the ground. The mammoth struggled to keep its balance, and as Gina watched the process of the mammoth slowly being forced to the ground, she was reminded of two huge sumo wrestlers she had seen compete in Japan. Just as the one sumo slowly tossed the other wrestler out of the ring, so did Yukon slowly force the mammoth to the ground. Yukon tipped the mammoth slightly more to its right and the beast finally lost its balance and fell down. Yukon immediately pounced on the beast. His fangs tore into the mammoth's neck and his fist crashed repeatedly into its skull. The mammoth swung his head toward Yukon and his tusks struck Yukon and knocked the Yeti onto his side. The mammoth stumbled to his feet as blood gushed from his neck.

Yukon had just stood when the mammoth charged him again. Yukon was now prepared for the mammoth's speed and the Yeti stepped to the left just before the mammoth's tusks reached him. As the mammoth was passing by Yukon, the Yeti dug his claws into the side of the beast's head and neck. Yukon held on for a few seconds as the mammoth pulled him across the snow-covered terrain. After several seconds, the mammoth's pace began to slow down and finally the beast fell to its knees beneath the fury of Yukon's assault. Yukon pushed the mammoth onto its side and then he used his fangs to tear out what remained of the mammoth's neck. Blood sprayed across Yukon's face and chest giving his white coat a red hue. Gina watched as Yukon then began to devour the dead mammoth.

The young anthropologist shook her head in awe at the battle that she had just witnessed. The mammoth weighed several tons, and not only was Yukon able to overpower it, he was able to maneuver around the creature with ease. The Yeti was amazing and deadly at the same time. Seeing the monster in action had only reaffirmed Gina's decision not to call for help. She was sure that any attempt to rescue her would only result in more members of her team dying.

Yukon fed off the dead mammoth for roughly a half an hour before tearing off a large chuck of meat and then heading back to the cave where he had left Gina. Yukon entered the cave and tossed the chunk of bloody mammoth meat at Gina's feet. Gina understood that Yukon wanted her to eat. She was not nearly hungry enough to eat the raw mammoth but as Yukon growled and gestured in the direction of the meat Gina remembered how Jun-Tuk had told her that the women who appeased the Yeti were those who came back alive. Gina scooped up a piece of raw mammoth, closed her eyes and then tossed it into her mouth. She nearly gagged but she finally managed to force herself to swallow a piece of the mammoth. She then nodded to Yukon in appreciation of his efforts. The Yeti snarled back at her then he picked her up and walked back out into the valley.

CHAPTER 7

Rodgers finally had the team ready to embark on the rescue mission. There were a dozen snowmobiles heading into the valley. Each snow mobile would carry two riders, meaning that more than half of the people who comprised the initial expedition would be part of the rescue team. Most of team consisted of graduate students who had taken basic first responder classes. Aside from Rodgers and Gordon, there were a few amateur hunters on the team. Rodgers had the amateur hunters take rifles or shotguns with them but he kept most of the team unarmed because he did want inexperienced people handling a weapon under a potentially stressful situation. Those who were unarmed carried other vital equipment such as tents, flares, medical supplies, and communications equipment.

Gordon was giving out the final orders to the team members as they were mounting their snowmobiles. "I only want certified people to carry weapons. We are going to move in two groups. Those of us who can use the rifles will move in a circle around the first responders. If you are not cleared to use a rifle then do not exit the inner circle unless if I give you the express permission to do so. I don't care if you see Professor Murella bleeding to death. Do not leave the inner circle unless I give you permission. Is that clear?" The hunter stared at the gathered team members with a look of superiority on his face. "Furthermore, we are likely to encounter strange and dangerous animals like the Yeti that took Professor Murella. This monster and the other beasts that we are likely to encounter in the valley are not typical animals. They are monsters. They will kill us without a second thought. Professor Murella does not want more lives to be lost in this rescue mission and neither do I. If we see any of these beasts, our policy will be to shoot first and ask questions later. I am going into that valley with over twenty men and women and I plan on leaving with that many. If there is anyone who has problem with the way I am running things then get the hell off of my team because you are putting the lives of everyone else at risk."

Rodgers was standing next to one of the snowmobiles like he was an Old West sheriff standing next to a horse and addressing a posse who were about to pursue a bunch of thieves. Henry could see that the man was on a power trip and thinking mainly of only bagging some rare trophies for himself. Everyone else saw this journey into the valley as a rescue mission but Rodgers saw it as a hunting trip. Henry was good at realizing how group dynamics worked. Rodgers was blowhard but he was also a charismatic speaker. If he did not do something to change the groups' perception of Rodgers, they would follow him into the valley and blindly carry out any order that he gave.

Henry didn't give Rodgers the chance to continue to spread his rhetoric to the gathered graduate students. He walked up next to Rodgers, and as subtly as possible, took the hunter's power over the group away from him. "Mr. Rodgers is right. It will be dangerous when we enter that valley. We will run into all kinds of strange and dangerous creatures that we are not familiar with and we do not know how they will react." Henry took a deep breath of cold air as he prepared to put his faith in a man he had only met a few days ago to save the love of his life. "Luckily, we have a man here who is accustomed to seeing these animals. He is Jun-Tuk, a native of these lands and a lifelong hunter himself. Mr. Rodgers has put together an excellent plan for entering and traversing the valley. When we are in the valley, we will follow the lead of Mr. Rodgers and he shall operate under the guidance of Jun-Tuk." Henry pointed to the old man. "With the skills of the greatest hunter in the world, under the guidance of a hunter who has unprecedented knowledge of this area and the animals that inhabit it, we will not only find and rescue my wife but we will learn a great deal about the greatest scientific discovery of the last two hundred years! Now quickly to your snowmobiles! We need to get into that valley before nightfall!" The graduate students were motivated by Henry's speech. They cheered and ran to the snowmobiles.

Rodgers grabbed Henry by the arm. "What in the hell is this, Henry? There is no way that I am going to follow the lead of that savage. We agreed that I would lead this team!"

Henry pulled his arm away from the hunter. "We agreed that you would coordinate the efforts to get the team prepared to head out. I am still in charge of the expedition and Jun-Tuk knows more about what's in that valley than you do. I am going to trust in him to get us and Gina out of there alive."

Rodgers shouted at Henry, "If you think that I am going to let the damn Eskimo lead us to our deaths then you are delusional!"

Henry shrugged. "Look Rodgers, I could really use your expertise in there but if don't want to follow Jun-Tuk's lead then you can stay here but just remember two things. First, Gina and I are the people who sign the checks, so if you want to stay here that's your call but I will stop paying you as of today. Also, if neither of us returns from that valley then no one will be signing your checks and you won't get paid at all. So it may be in your best interest to go into the valley with us to make sure that you get paid when you go home. The choice is totally up to you."

Henry mounted a snowmobile and Jun-Tuk climbed on behind him. Henry revved the engine and then he started off in the direction of the valley. The rest of the rescue team followed Henry as he drove across the frozen tundra. Rodgers cursed at Henry and then he too climbed onto a snowmobile and drove off in the direction of the valley.

Gina kept her body as compact as possible in Yukon's grip. She was well aware that were it not for the Yeti's body heat, even with her thermal gear she would have frozen to death. As she was trapped within the Yukon's hand enduring both his strength and the bitter cold, she continued to do her best to study the monster. The stamina of the creature was astounding. After fighting the mammoth, Yukon continued to trek across the valley at a fantastic speed. Based on the position of the sun, Gina was fairly sure that they were still heading further south. What she no idea about though was where exactly Yukon was taking her. This thought had no sooner crossed her mind than Yukon once more veered to the base of the mountain range that made up the edge of the valley.

Gina thought the Yukon might have been heading for another cave to rest but then she heard a splashing sound coming from the Yeti's feet. Gina looked down to see a thin stream of water moving across the snow. The Yeti continued to walk through the thin stream until it began to widen and become deeper.

Gina could see steam rising out of the water and she guessed that there must have been a hot stream that kept the water from freezing. She surmised that this stream served as a water source for the animals in the valley. Once the water was deep enough that Yukon could place his entire head in the water he put Gina down on the frozen bank of the stream, fell to his knees, and then he began drinking the life-giving fluid from the stream. Gina realized that she had no idea when she would have water available to her again. She could live for two weeks with minimal food but without water she would die from dehydration in a matter of days. Like the monster next to her, Gina also fell to her knees and took several deep mouthfuls of water.

Gina was drinking her fill when Yukon quickly pulled his head from the stream and began searching the surrounding area. Gina could not see anything but she heard a loud growl that sounded like a cougar. Yukon roared in return and then stepped in front of Gina. Gina's heart was racing as she peered out from behind the Yeti's leg. Yukon could see whatever was there but all that Gina could see was the snow. Then she saw a patch of snow suddenly move forward. She focused her eyes to see that it was not the snow itself moving, but rather something that was blending in with the snow. It was at the moment that Gina realized exactly what was moving toward her. She could see a large feline-like body with canine teeth that extend at least two feet from its upper jaws out of its mouth. Gina immediately realized two things. The first was that the saber-toothed cats in the valley had evolved to the point where their coats were white to help them blend into the snow. This camouflage would help them approach their prey just as snow leopard's white coat did a hare or a deer. As she started at the cat's long saber-like teeth, the second thing that she knew was exactly what had killed Jun-Tuk's daughter.

The saber-toothed cat stalked forward a few more steps then the monster crouched down as if it was going to pounce. The cat stood perfectly still and stared at Yukon. Gina could see the fur on Yukon's back bristling as anger and adrenaline coursed through the Yeti's body. Gina was transfixed by the stare down as she waited to see who would make the first move. The saber-toothed cat was by far the largest cat that Gina had ever seen. The beast stood over six feet tall and it was at least twelve-feet long. At a quick glance, Gina surmised that the predator was about half the size and weight of Yukon.

It was the fact that all of her senses were in a heightened state that helped Gina to hear the snarl behind her. Gina didn't think; she just reacted on instinct and dove to her left. She had no sooner landed in the snow than a second saber-toothed cat with a furry mane pounced onto Yukon's left calf and buried its claws into the Yeti's leg. Yukon howled in pain then he quickly swung his right hand toward the back of his leg and backhanded the saber-toothed cat off his leg before the cat could drive its long fangs into him. Yukon turned back toward the cat in front of him to see the beast pouncing at him. The first cat landed on Yukon's chest and used its claws to latch itself onto the Yeti. The first cat had no mane and Gina figured that it was a female and that the cat with a mane was a male.

The female cat lifted her head up as she prepared to drive her long canines into Yukon's heart but before she could bring her head forward, Yukon swatted the female off his chest. The female landed to the right of Gina. She looked at the female for a moment before the male jumped at her from her right. The male was in mid-air when Yukon's leg connected with the cat's ribs and sent the male flying to the right of Gina. Yukon stepped in front of Gina and turned his head to the female. The Yeti threw his arms out in a threating gesture and roared at the female cat. Gina knew that she would only live as long as Yukon could protect her from the saber toothed cats. She looked to her right to see the male regaining its footing.

The cats seemed to favor the method of leaping at Yukon one at time so that while the first cat took the brunt of Yukon's counter attack, the second cat had a free shot to injure the Yeti. Yukon was facing the female who was crouched down and ready to pounce. Gina took a quick moment to look to her right to see the male crouching down as well. Yukon was her protector but she also had to be aware that the Yeti might accidently crush her as he was attempting to fight off the two cats. She decided that she needed to time her movement with those of the cats. The female cat sprung at Yukon. The cat was still in the air when Yukon backhanded the female in the ribs and sent her flying away from both himself and Gina. Yukon had no sooner stuck the female than the male went to pounce on the Yeti's left leg. At the exact moment that the male jumped, Gina turned and ran, putting some distance between herself and the primordial battle taking place in front of her.

Yukon spun around and dug his own claws into the male cat's back, but before he could pull the male off his leg, the female landed on the Yeti's back and drove her claws into Yukon's shoulder blades. Gina thought the Yeti was about to meet his end when to her astonishment the primate changed tactics. Yukon threw himself to the ground then he started rolling across the snow away from Gina. The soft snow from the storm the night before helped to keep the saber-toothed cats from being crushed under Yukon's weight but it did force them to release their claws from the Yeti's flesh.

Yukon stood and turned to find the two cats standing next to each other and staring at him. The Yeti roared and once more threw his arms out to his sides. It seemed to Gina that the Yeti had the upper hand now that he would not have to deal with simultaneous attacks from the front and from behind. The Yeti roared again at the cats but they simply turned away from Yukon and looked at Gina. She cursed herself for being too caught up in the battle to realize that the cats were now between her and Yukon. Gina didn't think about her next move. She simply turned and did her best to run away from the cats through the ice and snow.

The saber-toothed cats took off after Gina and they were quickly gaining ground. Yukon did not try to pursue the cats. Instead, the Yeti bent down and began digging in the snow. Gina's lungs burned from the cold air that she was breathing in and she felt her right hamstring tighten up on her. The pulled muscle caused her to fall to the ground. She turned around to see the saber-toothed cats coming toward her, but behind the cats she could see Yukon standing up from the snow with a large chunk of ice in hands. The Yeti lifted the block of ice above his head then he threw it at the cats. The cats were less than ten feet away from Gina when the block of ice came crashing down on top of them.

The ice shattered on top of the cats as it forced both predators to the ground. Gina crawled backward as she watched the two stunned cats trying to stand up while Yukon sprinted toward them. The female cat had regained her feet when Yukon ran up next to her. The Yeti lifted his fist over his head then he quickly brought it straight down into the female's back. Gina heard a loud snap that she was sure was the female's spine. The female's limp body fell into the snow. Yukon lifted his massive foot up and then brought it down onto the female's head crushing her skull.

The male reared up and latched his claws onto the Yeti's hip. The male was tearing into the Yeti until Yukon wrapped his arms around the male's midsection. Yukon lifted the male over his head and then he tossed the male in the opposite direction of Gina. The male slid across the ice and snow for several feet before he was able to stop his momentum and regain his footing. Gina was still sitting in the snow, and despite the fact that her body was freezing, she could not take her eyes off the sight before her. The two prehistoric monsters were staring at each other preparing to engage in battle once again. The pure white fur of both monsters was streaked and matted with the bright red blood of both themselves and their opponent.

Yukon roared at the saber-toothed cat and the feline growled in response then sprang at the Yeti. The quicker cat once more managed to dig its claws into the Yeti's hip. The cat pulled his head back to plunge it into the primate's leg. Before the cat could bring its head forward Yukon's left hand wrapped around the cat's neck and held it still. Yukon reached down with his right hand, grabbed one of the cat's long canines, and with a turn of his wrist, the Yeti snapped the long weapon out of the cat's mouth. Yukon continued to hold the cat in his grip as he lifted the broken tooth over his head then plunged the cat's own tooth into his back. Yukon then forced the cat to the ground with his left hand while repeatedly striking the predator with his right fist. Gina watched in horror as Yukon continued to pound on the saber-toothed cat long after it had perished. Yukon did not cease his brutal attack until the remains of the male cat were little more than a pool of slush and blood. With his opponents defeated, the Yeti stood and looked at Gina. The Yeti's normally white fur was now almost entirely red and blood soaked. The Yeti threw his arms out and roared at the valley proclaiming his victory.

Once Yukon had finished roaring, Gina could feel the adrenaline in her body wearing off. Without the rush of adrenaline, she could now feel the cold that gripped her body. The only source of warmth available to her was Yukon himself. Like a toddler approaching her father, Gina walked over to Yukon with her arms open in a gesture for the monster to pick her up. Yukon looked down at Gina for a moment then he scooped her up in his warm and bloody hand. As soon as Yukon's fingers wrapped around Gina, she immediately felt her body warm up. Despite the blood that was soaking into her outer layer of clothing, Gina pulled her legs up toward her chest and slouched down as low as she could. She was trying to get as much of her body and in particular her fingers and toes into the warm palm of Yukon's hand.

With Gina safely in his grip, the Yeti took one last look at the vanquished cats and then he continued his journey farther south.

CHAPTER 8

Henry gripped the controls to his snowmobile with such force that his hands were shaking. He had the vehicle moving at full speed but he kept pushing the accelerator as hard as he could, as if by doing so he could will the machine to move faster. All that he could think about was how the monster had a several hour head start over them into a valley that they had never seen before. Those thoughts coupled with the fact that the monster took Gina out into subzero temperatures during a blizzard all added to Henry's concern for his wife.

When the valley came into view, Henry leaned forward and pushed down on the accelerator even harder. He maneuvered the snowmobile at full speed through several of the large boulders that dotted the entrance to the valley. The snowmobile went up the incline into the valley and launched itself into the air when it reached the apex of the valley pass.

The snowmobile hit the snow of the valley and Henry was about to take off in an eastern direction when Jun-Tuk tapped him on the shoulder. "We must wait for the others. We have greater safety in numbers and we must also determine which direction the Yeti took your wife in. This valley is large. If we simply move around it without a definite direction, we will move to far away from the valley pass to make our way back out. If we become lost in the valley, it will be only a few days before the animals or the elements end our lives."

Henry nodded in reply. Jun-Tuk was right. As anxious as Henry was to rescue Gina, he knew that keeping a level head and following a plan would be the most effective way to locate his wife.

A moment later, Rodgers and the rest of the rescue team pulled up next to Henry and Jun-Tuk. "Henry, you have to wait for everyone else before you just take off. We need to move as a group if we are going to be successful." Henry nodded silently in reply to the hunter. Rodgers returned the nod and then looked at

Gordon. "Do we have anything from either the radio or the transmitter that Professor Murella took with her?"

Gordon looked at the transmitter to see that it was still not receiving any information. He then put the radio up to his mouth and turned it on. "Professor Murella, this is Tony Gordon, do you copy?" There was no answer, and after waiting ten seconds, he spoke into the radio again, "Professor Murella, this is Tony Gordon, do you copy?" Once again, there was no reply. Gordon looked toward Rodgers. "Nothing. It seems as if Professor Murella still has her communication equipment turned off."

Rodgers shrugged then he directed his attention to Jun-Tuk. "Well, what direction do we head from here?"

Jun-Tuk didn't wait for Henry to translate. He knew what the hunter was asking him to do. Jun-Tuk climbed off the snowmobile and walked roughly thirty feet to the right side of the valley pass. Once he reached the steepest section of the mountain on which he could still stand upright, he bent down and took a long look at the snow around him. After staring at the snow, he stood and he began walking back down the slope of the mountain and into the valley. He walked in a wide arch from one side of the valley pass to the other. As he walked, he kept his head down, constantly staring at the snow. When he reached the right side of the valley pass, he climbed that as well. He had walked up about halfway up the base of the mountain when he suddenly stopped and bent down. The old man stood and then he began taking large steps in a southern direction. He took five steps that covered the maximum length of his stride. He took five more steps and then bent down again and looked at the snow. He nodded and then looked toward Henry. "The Yeti took your wife in a southern direction." He pointed to the snow. "There are indents in the snow that take five large steps for me to cover. They are the steps of a beast that walks on two legs. The snow filled in most of the tracks but the Yeti is heavy and his feet are large. As long as we keep the dog-less sleds from moving over the tracks, I believe that I can track him."

Henry translated for the rest of the group, and after hearing what Jun-Tuk had to say, both Gordon and Rodgers walked over to where the old man was to inspect his findings. Gordon bent down to examine the snow, and when Jun-Tuk pointed to the indentations, Gordon nodded affirmatively then returned to his snowmobile. Rodgers was skeptical of the native's ability to track an animal, but when Jun-Tuk showed him the evidence, he begrudgingly had to admit that he concurred with the old man's findings. Rodgers looked at the rest of the rescue team and shouted, "We have tracks that are heading in a southern direction. We will reform our circle with Jun-Tuk taking point on the right side of the circle nearest to the tracks. It is important that we don't run over the tracks themselves." Rodgers looked specifically at Henry. "We also need to maintain a moderate speed. Moving faster won't help us or Professor Murella if we lose the tracks and get lost in the valley."

Henry nodded as Jun-Tuk was climbing back onto his snowmobile. Satisfied that everyone understood his orders, Rodgers climbed back onto his snowmobile and the group started following the tracks in pursuit of the Yeti. The group followed the tracks for over twenty minutes when Rodgers signaled for them to stop. The hunter stared out across the ice at a large brown creature that was staring back at him. Rodgers slowly stood up to get a better look at the creature. It was standing roughly two hundred yards away from the group. The creature stood on four feet and it was covered in brown fur. The creature was not as large as the mammoths that Rodgers had seen the day before. This creature was slightly smaller than the mammoths. The beast was about fifteen feet long and roughly stood ten feet at the top of its shoulders. The creature's face was long and it ended in a huge brown horn.

Henry pulled up next to Rodgers. "What are we stopping for?"

Rodgers pointed out at the brown mass. "If I didn't know any better, I would say that's a rhinoceros."

Gordon and Dana pulled up on the other side of Rodgers as Henry took a look through his binoculars. "It's a woolly rhino. It's the Ice Age equivalent of our modern rhino just as the wooly mammoth is the Ice Age equivalent to our modern elephant. Just like the mammoth and the elephant, the wooly rhino is larger and stronger than the modern version."

Dana was sitting behind Gordon on one of the snowmobiles. She slid off the vehicle and walked over toward Henry. "I've only ever seen rhino's on TV and at the zoo, but I am sure that I have heard they are extremely aggressive. Maybe we should just move on before that thing thinks that we are a threat to it."

Rodgers started walking to edge of the snowmobiles closer to the wooly rhino. When he reached the end of the snowmobiles he pulled his rifle off his shoulder and dropped to one knee.

He was taking aim at the animal when Henry shouted at him. "Rodgers, what the hell are you doing? That thing isn't bothering us. Just leave it alone."

Rodgers shook his head. "That head of that thing alone will make me a millionaire. Then I won't have to concern myself with whether or not you or your wife signs my checks." Before Henry could respond, Rodgers lifted his rifle and fired at the beast. The shot rang out and echoed across the barren terrain. The bullet struck the rhino and ricocheted off its thick hide. The beast snorted, turned toward the snowmobiles, lowered its head, and charged the rescue team.

The beast was moving with incredible speed for its size. Henry screamed, "Move people! Get the hell away from that thing!" Most of the rescue team jumped onto their snowmobiles. Dana climbed onto Gordon's snowmobile and she wrapped her arms around the young hunter as they sped off. As everyone else was fleeing, Rodgers maintained his position and fired another shot at the rhino. The second shot caught the charging rhino in the shoulder and managed to penetrate its tough skin. The enraged beast snorted and continued to charge. Rodgers quickly realized that he would not be able to bring down the charging animal. He stood up and turned to run for his snowmobile. He took two steps and walked directly into the path of one of the oncoming snowmobiles. The team members veered to the right to avoid Rodgers and they crashed into a second snowmobile causing both vehicles to fall onto their sides and sending four team members tumbling through the snow.

Rodgers took one look at the fallen people, then he ran to his snowmobile, and jumped onto to it. The hunter sped away as the unarmed graduate students tried desperately to lift up their snowmobiles. Henry was speeding away when Jun-Tuk tapped Henry on the shoulder and shouted for him to turn around. Henry looked over his shoulder to see the wooly rhino quickly closing in on the graduate students. Henry looked over at Gordon and shouted, "Gordon, we have people down!" He then turned his snowmobile around and started heading for the graduate students.

Gordon didn't waste time responding. He turned his snowmobile around and followed Henry back toward the graduate students with Dana holding tightly onto his waist. The wooly rhino had almost reached the graduate students when Gordon yanked his rifle off his shoulder and fired a desperate shot at the charging beast. The bullet struck the animal in the stomach, and while it managed to penetrate the animal's hide, it didn't slow down the charging monster. The wooly rhino slammed into the downed snowmobile with the force of a runaway train. The snowmobile went sliding across the snow as two of the students were trampled to death under the feet of the charging behemoth. Henry watched helplessly as his students were crushed into nothing more than a red and white pulp beneath the wooly rhino's feet. The remaining two students were screaming in terror and running toward the snowmobile when the rhino turned to them and charged. The beast lowered his head and used his horn to toss one of the students into the air. The screaming young woman flew twenty feet in the air before landing on her head, instantly crushing her skull and breaking her spine. The last surviving student was roughly fifty feet from Henry when the wooly rhino's massive horn entered her back and exploded out of her chest. The woman was screaming in agony until a gunshot sounded and her head exploded. Henry looked to his right to see Gordon holding his rifle in his hand. The hunter was frantically signaling Henry to turn around. Henry nodded and spun his snowmobile around less than ten feet from the wooly rhino. From the corner of his eye, Henry saw the wooly rhino shake his head to send the corpse of the graduate student flying off his horn and into the snow.

Henry had just completed his turn when the wooly rhino charged his snowmobile. Gordon's snowmobile was just ahead of Henry and the rest of the rescue team was in the distance far ahead of them and still speeding away. Henry was pushing his vehicle to the limit and even with that he could hear the monster gaining on him. He feared that at any second the beast would upend his snowmobile and end his life.

Henry dared to take one last look over his shoulder to see the wooly rhino slowing down and then turning away from the fleeing snowmobiles. After moving at full speed for fifteen minutes, the rescue team finally came to a stop to regroup and assess their current situation. Henry could see Rodgers pulling his snowmobile to a stop in the group ahead of him. Henry pulled up alongside of Rodgers then he jumped off his snowmobile. The normally calm Henry grabbed Rodgers by the shoulder and then he punched the hunter in the jaw. Rodgers stumbled backward as Henry yelled at him. "Those kids are dead because of you! I told you to leave that rhino alone! If you hadn't been thinking of making yourself rich, those kids would still be alive!"

Rodgers sneered. "And if you hadn't convinced Princeton to send you down here, your wife wouldn't be in the clutches of a Yeti."

Henry went to strike the hunter again when Gordon stepped between the two men. "This isn't helping. We need to decide what we are going to do and move on."

Henry nodded. "Okay, from now on, Gordon is in charge of making decisions when we come across the creatures in this valley." He turned to Gordon. "Don't fire on anything unless we have to in self-defense."

Gordon nodded at Henry as Dana walked up beside him. "Thank you for sparing that girl from a slow and painful death."

Gordon shrugged. "I couldn't save her but the least that I could do was to end her suffering."

Dana hugged him. "You did the right thing."

As Dana was hugging Gordon, Henry climbed back onto his snowmobile and shouted, "Alright everyone, there is nothing else that we can do here. Let's keep moving before some other monster comes along."

CHAPTER 9

Gina had passed out as the Yeti continued to carry her farther south. She was still half asleep when she felt a warmth emanating from beside her. She opened her eyes slowly, and through blurred vision, she saw an orange color to her right. She blinked twice to focus her vision and the fire that was burning beside her came into view. Gina was disoriented from the cold and she tried to survey her surroundings to see where she was. She quickly realized that wherever she was, it was dark. The only available light was coming from the fire next to her. She looked up to make out several stalactite reaching down at her from above. She blinked her eyes several more times to realize that she was inside of another cave. Gina sat up and when she did so she was immediately hit by the smell of the Yeti. She stood up and looked to her left to see Yukon sleeping roughly sixty feet away from her. When she saw how far away from her that Yukon was sleeping, she realized the vast size of the cave that she was in. The gargantuan Yukon was sleeping a good distance away from her and she still could not determine where the opening to the cave was. By using the Yeti to scale, she could see that the twenty-five foot tall Yeti had plenty of head clearance in the cave. She could also see that the cave was at least three times as wide as Yukon was tall. At a quick assessment, she guessed that the area of the cave that she was in was at least forty-feet high and seventy-five feet wide. She couldn't even begin to guess at the depth of the immense formation.

Gina noticed that she was sweating and she thought that it was because she was next to the fire. As the thought of how hot she was crossed her mind, it immediately brought two other questions to the forefront of her concerns. The first concern was that it was far too hot in the cave for the small fire to be heating the vast cavern. Gina guessed that the cave they were in must be near some underground source of heat such as magma. The second question that had entered her mind was *who exactly had started the fire?* In her brief time with Yukon, she had learned that the monster was at least as intelligent as a gorilla or a chimpanzee, but she doubted that the beast had the ability to purposely build a fire. She briefly considered that perhaps, in her near frozen and exhausted state that she created the fire herself, but she quickly pushed the thought aside. Gina looked at the fire, and from what she could tell, the fire was being fueled by a mixture of bones and dung. She shook her head and spoke out loud, "I am pretty sure that I was in no condition to make a fire. I am also sure that even with as tired as I was that I would have remembered building a fire."

Gina started walking around the cave as she continued to talk to herself, "The only animal in the history of the planet that has ever been known to create fire is man." As Gina spoke the words aloud, she stopped walking and her eyes opened wide. "That means that there are other people here." Gina's mind began racing as she considered the implications of her hypothesis. "That either means that there is another missing tribe that knowingly shares a cave with a Yeti or..." Gina stopped in mid-sentence. She couldn't bring herself to say what she was thinking aloud. Her entire body shook as she realized the other possibility of why humans would be sharing a cave with a Yeti. Based on the wounds to Jun-Tuk's daughter, and the saber-toothed cat attack that she had witnessed, Gina had assumed that the young women who Yukon had taken from Jun-Tuk's tribe that he did not return had died. Gina had never considered that Yukon might have kept some of the women in his cave.

Gina's mind was racing at the thought of women being held captive by Yukon in this hellish valley. She yelled out in ancient Incan, "Hello, is there anyone in here?" Her shout echoed through the cave several times before it finally died out. Then Gina heard two sounds in reply. The first sound confused her and the second sound terrified her. The first sound that Gina thought that she heard, was a crying baby that came from deeper in the cave. That sound was quickly drowned out by a terrifying roar that seemed to come from behind where Yukon was sleeping.

Everything around Gina suddenly started moving in a blur. First, Yukon stood and roared, then a young woman who looked as if she was from the same tribe that Jun-Tuk was from, came running out from deeper in the cave. The woman ran up to Gina, and started pleading with her to be quiet. A second loud roar from what Gina guessed was the direction of the entrance to the cave echoed throughout the cavern. Yukon roared again then the massive Yeti started walking in the direction of the other roaring creature. Every sensible fiber of Gina's being was urging her to run deeper into the cave and away from the new creature. Conversely, the scientist in her forced her to run over to the area where Yukon had been sleeping in order to see what manner of beast was threatening her and challenging the Yeti.

Gina saw a large stalagmite that would hide her from the view of whatever it was that had made its way into the cave. She crouched down behind it as the woman from Jun-Tuk's tribe continued to make arm motions for Gina to follower her. Gina was interested in hearing the woman's story but currently she was much more fascinated in seeing what manner of creature would dare to challenge Yukon. The roar was too deep to have come from another saber-toothed cat. Whatever this creature was, it much larger than the cats that she had come across earlier. Gina peeked out from behind the stalagmite and she was finally able to see the entrance to the cave. She could see Yukon walking toward the entrance. See stuck her head out a little farther from behind the stalagmite to see a huge form lumber into the cave entrance. At first, all that Gina could see was that the animal walked on all fours but she was not able to make out any details that revealed exactly what type of creature the animal was. The beast that was entering the cave roared again and then it stood up on two feet. As the monster's entire form was silhouetted by the sun light pouring in from behind it, Gina was finally able to make out what type of animal was making its way into the cave.

Gina had seen several species of bear in her travels. She was very familiar with large members of the species, such as grizzly bears and polar bears. She had beheld the huge animals both in controlled settings like zoos and in the field while she was on various expeditions. While both grizzly bears and polar bears were large, the bear that was making its way into the cave would have dwarfed even the largest member of any known species of bear. When the bear was standing on its hind legs, it was taller than Yukon meaning that the beast was somewhere around thirty feet tall. Based on the other prehistoric animals that Gina had seen, she guessed that the animal must have been some species of large cave bear.

The cave bear roared again, then it dropped back to all fours and began running toward Yukon. Yukon threw his arms out in front of himself and roared in return at the bear, both warning the attacking animal and accepting its challenge at the same time. The bear drove its head and shoulders into Yukon's waist, knocking the Yeti into a sitting position. The cave bear quickly moved forward and attempted to use his body to pin Yukon to the ground. As the cave bear approached him, Yukon pulled his knees in and put his large feet against the cave bear's chest. Yukon then pushed with his legs and sent the cave bear tumbling back toward the cave entrance.

The bear quickly regained control of his momentum and once again the massive creature stood on its hind legs. It roared at Yukon again, but instead of returning the roar, the Yeti lowered his head and drove his shoulder into the cave bear's midsection. The force of the impact sent the cave bear crashing into the wall of the cave. Before the cave bear could right himself, Yukon slammed his body into the body of the bear. Gina watched as Yukon hammered the bear with alternating blows from his fists. The Yeti had struck the bear four times before the cave bear was able to swipe Yukon across the face with his claw. The cave bear's claw slash caused Yukon to cease his attack and take a step backward. The cave bear took a step forward, wrapped his arms around Yukon, and dug his claws into the Yeti's back. The cave bear then bit down into the Yeti's shoulder, causing even more red blood to soak Yukon's white coat.

Yukon roared in pain then the Yeti wrapped his powerful arms around the lower part of the cave bear's ribcage. The two beasts were locked in a test of strength. As Gina watched the two monsters, she recalled the awesome display of power and the intelligent use of leverage that Yukon had exhibited when he had toppled the wooly mammoth. As she thought about how Yukon had forced the mammoth to the ground, she had no doubt that the Yeti would overpower the cave bear as well. Gina's prediction quickly came to fruition as Yukon shifted his left leg backward and pushed down with his right arm in a move that caused the cave bear to slam into the cave floor. Yukon roared then he began stomping on the neck and shoulder of the invading cave bear.

Gina was transfixed by the battle to the point where she did not notice that the other woman in the cave had crept up behind her. The woman placed her hand on Gina's shoulder and Gina screamed in surprise. She turned around to see the woman who said to her in ancient Incan, "Come with me, please! If the cave bear wins this battle, he will kill us if we stay in the open." Gina's scream had also caught Yukon's attention and caused the Yeti to stop stomping on the cave bear in order to see if Gina was in need of his assistance. The cave bear took full advantage of the Yeti's momentary lack of focus on the battle. The cave bear bit into Yukon's calf and pulled on it, causing the Yeti to once more fall to the ground. Gina watched Yukon's skull bounced off the cave floor when the creature hit the ground. The Yeti was stunned and reached up with his hands to grab his head.

The cave bear once again quickly moved forward in another attempt to pin Yukon beneath his body. The disoriented Yukon was unable to use his feet to catch the cave bear and the animal's entire weight pressed down onto the Yeti. The cave bear opened his jaws and he went to tear out the Yeti's throat when Yukon's hands reached out and grabbed onto the bear's throat. Gina could see Yukon's sharp claws digging into the bear's neck and she knew she was witnessing the end of this clash of the titans. The bear continued to try and reach Yukon's throat as the Yeti squeezed the cave bear's neck. Yukon's entire body was shaking as he fought to both keep the bear from killing him and at the same time strangling the beast.

Just as Yukon had done when the mammoth had him pinned to the ground, the Yeti was once more fighting his way back to his feet. Yukon's incredible strength was slowly forcing the head and body of the cave bear away from his throat. After a few seconds, Yukon had managed to fully extend his arms. Blood was spurting from the cave bear's neck as Yukon continued to force his claws deeper into the monster's throat. When the majority of the cave bear's weight was pushed off him, Yukon stood up and released his grip. The exhausted bear shook his head and Gina was sure that the creature was choking on his own blood. The damage that

Yukon had wrought on the bear had caused its own blood pour into its lungs. The cave bear was on all fours and it started to stagger away from Yukon and toward the cave entrance. Yukon stepped forward and kicked the fleeing cave bear causing the dying creature to fall flat on its face in front of the cave entrance. The cave bear was taking its last breaths at the entrance to the cave when Yukon walked over to the beast. The Yeti reached down and grabbed the bear. In another show of tremendous strength, Yukon lifted the cave bear over his head as he stepped out of the cave. The Yeti roared then he threw the cave bear down the steep slope that led up to the cave entrance.

Yukon threw his arms out in front of himself and roared proclaiming his victory to the world. Gina and the woman from the cave were still watching from behind the stalactite when Gina asked aloud in English, "Why did he throw the bear out of the cave? He could have just left it there to die."

The woman from the cave asked Gina what she meant in ancient Incan. Gina repeated the question in the woman's native language. The woman from the cave shook her head. "The Yeti god knows not to leave dead things in the cave because it will attract the crawling demons."

Gina gave the woman a puzzled look. "You mean the saber-toothed cats?"

The woman shook her head again. "No, the crawling demons from deep inside the mountain. The crawling demons move like water and eat the living and the dead. They are attracted by dead things, and if they come as a large group, even the Yeti god would not be able to fight them off. The crawling demons from the cave cannot stand the cold. They will not venture out there to retrieve the dead beast." The women then pointed to Yukon. "Also, he does not like the taste of cave bear. I find the cave bear's meat too difficult for my stomach to digest. I suspect that the Yeti god has had a similar experience with bear meant when he has tried to eat it. He will leave the cave bear outside for the black flying demons. They can eat anything and they will remove the remains of the bear." Gina was about to ask the woman more questions about the *crawling demons from within the cave* when the sound of a baby screaming started to echo through cave.

The women motioned for Gina to follower her. "Come, the Yeti god will rest after his battle. We must attend to our child."

Gina was taken aback by the woman's comment. She repeated the woman's troubling words in English, "Our child?""

CHAPTER 10

After escaping the wooly rhino, the rescue team continued to follow the tracks of the Yeti. They had continued to head south until they saw three huge dark black shapes in the snow ahead of them. The dark figures were standing over a large red and brown mass lying in the snow. Gordon signaled for the team to come to a stop behind him. He turned around to Dana and she was so close to him that had they not had scarves wrapped around their faces, their lips would have touched. Dana was thankful that her scarf and dark snow goggles prevented Gordon from seeing her blushing.

The young hunter quickly apologized. "I am sorry, Doctor Summers." He was quiet for a moment and then he finally managed to say, "I was hoping that you could hand me my binoculars."

Dana reached into the carrying case strapped to the back of the snowmobile and handed the binoculars to Gordon. "Here you go, and you can call me Dana."

Gordon nodded. "Thank you, Dana."

Henry and Jun-Tuk pulled up next to Gordon, and Rodgers pulled his snowmobile to a stop a few feet behind them. Henry could hear the disgruntled Rodgers mumbling under his breath. Henry pushed any thoughts of the self-centered Rodgers aside and brought his own binoculars to his eyes. Henry was able to make out three huge birds of prey each standing nearly ten feet tall. The birds looked like some kind of cross-breed between a condor and a crow. Henry removed his binoculars form his eyes and directed his attention to Gordon. "If I had to guess, I would say that those things are teratorns. Again, I am no paleontologist, but giant birds that were similar in size to those things hunted our earliest human ancestors. They have a wingspan of about eighteen feet long. Skulls of early humans have been found all over the world with three huge holes poked into them. The prevailing belief is that the holes were caused from teratorns using their claws to crush the heads of their prey. They appear to be feeding on the remains of one of the mammoths that we saw earlier." He put his binoculars back into his carrying case as he sighed. "How do you think we should handle this situation?"

Gordon continued to look through his binoculars at the teratorns and the dead mammoth. "The Yeti tracks look like they lead to the cave up there and then back out again long after the snow storm had ended. The tracks coming out of the cave are much deeper and clearer than the first set of prints leading into the cave. From the look of the surrounding area, I would say that the Yeti killed that mammoth and then after eating a large portion of it, looks like he went back to the cave." Gordon stopped for a moment and then turned to Henry. "I can't say for sure, but if the monster went back to the cave after making the kill then he went back in there for something. It could be a sign that he went back to get Doctor Murella."

Henry's felt a wave of hope run through his body at the mere idea that his wife was alive and possibly in this area only a short time ago. Gordon looked back to the teratorns. "After exiting the cave, the Yeti tracks continue right past that dead mammoth and those teratorns. They are clearly scavenging off the remains of the mammoth. If they behave like modern birds of prey, they could very well attack a potential meal, especially if humans were once a part of their diet." Gordon motioned to Jun-Tuk. "Could you please ask Jun-Tuk if he or his people know anything about those birds and how they might react to humans?"

Henry asked Jun-Tuk if he knew anything about the birds. Jun-Tuk nodded and then he told Henry about his encounter with the *flying death birds* as he referred to them. "When I entered the valley to find my daughter, I tracked the Yeti for several hours before the flying death birds spotted me. The birds swooped down at me in an attempt to slay me. I hit one of the birds with my spear but the weapon was unable to inflict much damage on the creature. I managed to run from cave to cave until the birds lost interest in me. Without my spear, I returned to the valley entrance, and as I was leaving the valley, another of the flying death birds attempted to attack me. When I entered the valley pass, the creature flew straight up and away from me. I think that the mountain winds somehow keep the creatures from exiting the valley."

Henry repeated what Jun-Tuk had told him to Gordon. Gordon nodded. "We don't have any choice but to go past the teratorns. If we don't continue to follow the tracks, we may never find Doctor Murella. We will try to make a wide arch around the birds and then loop back to tracks. Let's hope that the birds are more interested in the dead mammoth than they are in us."

Gordon leaned back to his fellow passenger. "Dana, I want you to put my rifle in my lap in case I need to use it. Then keep a tight hold around my waist and keep your head low." He paused for a moment. "Don't worry, no matter what happens I will make sure that you are safe."

Dana squeezed Gordon hard, and at that moment, she wished that they were in some tropical setting where she wasn't wearing a scarf because it was the perfect opportunity to have kissed him.

A few feet away from them, Jun-Tuk spoke to Henry, "Keep your weapon ready. The flying death birds are ravenous. I suspect that we will not be able to give them a wide enough birth to prevent them from attacking." Henry nodded in reply then he revved his engine and started to arch around the teratorns. He knew that Gordon would gladly have led the team past the massive birds, but Henry felt the young hunter had already more than done his part. They had already lost two people in the attempt to rescue his wife. Henry was determined to do whatever he could to prevent any more of the brave volunteers from dying in the valley. Henry felt that if he could make himself the primary target for the teratorns that if they decided to attack then he would at least be keeping the birds' attention off the other rescue team members.

Henry rode his snowmobile at least two hundred yards wide to the left of the teratorns before he turned his vehicle back toward the mountain range and the Yeti tracks. Henry was no tracker, but he figured that once they were clear of the teratorns, Gordon could retake the lead position. Henry had his snowmobile moving at top speed as he moved parallel to the teratorns. He kept whispering to himself, "Please, please let the sound of the snowmobiles keep them at bay." Henry saw the teratorns looking up from the carrion before them to watch the snowmobiles. Henry continued to hope that the teratorns would just let them pass by. Henry had almost cleared the massive birds when he saw one of them take flight. The other two birds quickly joined the first bird as they took to the air as well.

Henry cursed as he tightened his grip on his rifle. Henry was astounded at the speed of the birds. They had managed to overtake the snowmobiles in a matter of seconds. Henry's thoughts switched from praying the teratorns would leave them alone to hoping that the birds were only curious about the strange new objects moving through their valley. Henry's hope quickly changed to horror when he heard a high-pitched scream from behind him. He turned his head around to see one of the snowmobiles fall to the ground as a team member was tossed from the back of it. The team member that was tossed from the snowmobile bounced off the frozen terrain like a tennis ball. Even to Henry, it was obvious that the young woman had died when she was thrown into the tundra. The scream of the team member who had been driving the snowmobile was cut short as the teratorn used its claw to puncture the young man's skull and slice his brain in half.

Henry heard gunshots from behind him. He turned his head around again briefly to see Gordon holding his rifle with one hand and firing at a teratorn as it was swooping down at another team member. Gordon had dropped to the back of the group. He had positioned himself there so that he could try to protect the other team members from the horrors above them. It seemed as if Gordon's bullets were slowing the teratorns down but they were not causing enough damage to kill any of the three birds. Henry cursed himself at first, thinking that if he wanted to protect people, he should have been the one in the back of the party. Then he remembered that Gordon was a much better shot that he was and that he had put Gordon in charge of the rescue operation for a reason. The stoic Gordon had probably wanted Henry to lead the group so that he could protect the team members from behind if he needed to.

Another gun shot was followed by a scream as a Gordon tried in vain to keep the giant birds from grabbing another team member. This time it was the young man riding on the back of a snowmobile who the bird had taken. The young man's skull was immediately crushed as the person who he had shared a snowmobile with a moment ago continued to drive his vehicle forward as quickly as he could. The rider moved up next to Henry. The anthropologist looked over at the young student just in time to see a teratorn grabbed the man off his snowmobile and carry him into the air. Henry thought to himself that at least that was the fourth person to die in the teratorn attack. Each of the horrible birds had killed at least one team member. Henry had thought that since all three of the horrible creatures now had something else to eat that the attack was over.

Henry realized that he was wrong about the attack being over when a huge bird-shaped shadow covered his snowmobile. Henry quickly shifted his snowmobile to the right and when the vehicle shifted over from its path the teratorn's claws clamped shut directly where Henry's head would have been. It dawned on Henry that the teratorns would kill the entire team. They would crush each of the team members' skulls and when everyone was dead only then would the teratorns feed on their bodies. Jun-Tuk arm shot past Henry's face and pointed back to the mountains. The old man screamed, "Head for one of the caves!"

Henry shifted his snowmobile back in the direction of the mountains, but instead of driving directly for them, he moved his vehicle in a zigzag pattern. He looked behind him to see the other team members following his lead. Henry had seen numerous movies where people moved in such a pattern in order to make it more difficult for a sniper to shoot them. He hoped that the same premise would apply to giant birds diving at him from overhead.

The teratorns continued to dive at the fleeing team members, but the erratic movements of the snowmobiles prevented the carnivorous birds from claiming any more of the rescue team. Henry pulled his snowmobile to a stop at the base of the cave. He directed Jun-Tuk to run up into the cave. Jun-Tuk ran toward the cave and Henry started firing at the huge birds as they continued to menace his friends and students. Henry could tell that he had hit one or the birds when it squawked and briefly increased its altitude. The effect was only temporary as after a brief second the teratorn was back in pursuit of the remaining team members. As people pulled their snowmobiles alongside Henry, he screamed for them to run up and into the cave.

Most of the remaining team members had made it to the base of the mountain and were making their way up to the cave when Rodgers pulled up alongside Henry. Only the snowmobile with Gordon and Dana and one other vehicle carrying two people on it were still trying to make their way to the base of the mountain. Seeing that four people were still in danger, Rodgers dismounted and began firing at the teratorns. Henry took aim at one of the birds, but when he pulled his trigger, all that he heard was a hollow click.

Rodgers yelled at Henry, "You are out of ammo! Grab the supply bag on the back of my snowmobile; it's got some extra bullets in it! Run up to the cave. I will cover Gordon and the others! When you get up there, quickly reload and then cover us as we make our way up there!" Rodgers continued to fire at the huge birds as Henry grabbed the supply bag and ran up to the cave. As Henry heard Rodgers continue to fire at the teratorns, he thought to himself that Rogers may have been self-centered and arrogant but no one could call the man a coward. Rodgers knew that by carelessly running during the wooly rhino attack that he had cost four people their lives. It seemed that he was now determined to try and rectify that mistake by saving four people.

Henry raced to the cave entrance. When he was just outside of the cave, he tried to reload his rifle. He quickly realized that he was not experienced enough with the rifle to reload it with his gloves on. Henry cursed then he tore his cloves off. He could feel the cold sting his hands the instant that his gloves came off. He knew that in the sub-zero temperatures he was in that he had less than a minute before frostbite started claiming his fingers. He worked as quickly as he could and he managed to load several bullets into the rifle before he couldn't stand the cold any longer.

With his gun reloaded and his gloves back on, Henry looked down at the base of the mountain. He saw Rodgers and Gordon maintaining a cover fire as Dana and the last two graduate students made their way up to the cave. When reached they mouth of the cave, Henry ran into the cave with them. As he entered the cave, Henry was immediately surprised at how warm the cave was. Henry guessed that there had to be at least a thirty degree difference in the cave entrance alone and the outside temperature.

He was angry at himself for not entering the cave before trying to reload his rifle and nearly costing himself several fingers. Henry's thoughts were focused back on the teratorns when Dana yelled at him, "Cover them! They are going to be killed out there!"

Henry dropped to one knee and aimed his rifle at an approaching teratorn. He pulled the trigger and he was pretty sure that he had hit the bird in the wing when it made a sharp turn to its left. When the two hunters heard the shot ring out from above them, they started running for the cave entrance. Another bird swooped down at Gordon and Rodgers. Henry didn't take time to aim his weapon; he simply fired it as quickly as he could. Henry wasn't sure if he had hit a vital area on the monster or if an accumulation of bullet wounds had finally caught up to the teratorn, but whatever the cause, the raptor quickly crashed into the snow. To make sure that the monster was dead, Henry fired one more shot at the downed bird. The teratorn lifted its head and screeched one final time before dying. Rodgers and Gordon climbed into the cave and Rodgers turned to Henry. "Good shot, Henry! I didn't think that there was a hunter in you, but you just bagged yourself one hell of a trophy!"

Henry was about to scream at Rodgers that he didn't give a damn about trophies but his attention was quickly called back to the front of the cave. One of the remaining teratorns flew directly up to the cave entrance. The bird flew into the huge cave and then it started flapping its wings and jabbing at Henry with its beak. The bird's talon moved quicker than Henry's eyes were able to see. He felt a pressure across his mid-section as he was pushed backward. Henry found himself looking at a blur of talons, beak, and feathers as the teratorn continued to move frantically as it tried to makes it way deeper into the cave.

Henry quickly reached his hand down to his mid-section and he felt a deep tear in his insulated coat. He continued to push his hand further into his stomach until he felt his T-shirt. Henry briefed a sigh of relief when he found that his T-shirt, and thankfully his stomach, were intact. Henry realized that if it were not for his heavy winter gear that the bird's claw would have eviscerated him. His mind was brought back to the terror at hand when the massive teratorn jumped forward a few more feet toward him.

Gordon yelled, "Henry, shoot! Gordon and I are still reloading!" Henry quickly pointed his rifle and fired at the teratorn at point blank range. The bird screeched in pain and hopped backward toward the opening to the cave. Gordon and Rodgers knelt down next to Henry. Gordon lifted Henry up to one knee. Gordon then immediately took control of the situation. He yelled to Henry and Rodgers, "On my mark, fire at the center of its chest! Three, two, one, fire!" The three rifles sounded off as one and their combined power caused the teratorn to tumble away from cave entrance.

The three men rushed to the front of the cave to see the last teratorn make a wide circle overhead and then dive toward the cave entrance. Gordon screamed again, "On my mark, aim for its head! Three, two, one, fire!" The three men fired in unison at the teratorn. The horrifying bird screeched and convulsed in midair before crashing into the mountain on the left side of the cave.

Henry was breathing hard as the adrenaline rush that had surged through his body started to wear off. He turned around to see the terrified students who had followed him on this expedition to rescue his wife. Several of his students, brilliant young men and women who had put themselves in his care, were now dead. Henry told himself that they had volunteered to go into the valley but they didn't know what they getting into and honestly neither did Henry. Henry knew that the deaths of those students were on his head. He would carry that burden with him for the rest of his life. He had been desperate to save his wife and in doing so he had put these people in danger.

Henry knew what he had to do. He took a deep breath and then he addressed the rescue team. "The deaths that have occurred here today are my fault. The words don't exist for me to tell you how sorry I am for bringing you into this valley. I can't rectify my mistake, but I can keep it from getting any worse. Tomorrow, Gordon will lead you back to the campsite outside of the valley. You will wait there for two more days. If by that time neither I nor Gina returns, you are to head home."

One of the graduate students spoke up, "Professor, we volunteered for this rescue mission. We are here on our own accord and we are going to go on with you on our own accord."

Henry shook his head. "I thank you all for your bravery, but you are my responsibility. I have failed you in my responsibility to ensure your safety because I was blinded by grief over what happened to my wife. Gina made it clear to not send a rescue party after her because she didn't want any more people to die. As usual, her perception of the situation was far more clear and accurate than mine." Henry took a deep breath and shrugged. "I can't even guarantee that you can make it back alive from this point, but I won't have you go any further." Henry waved his arm around the massive cave. "This cave is huge and it is warm. Gordon, Rodgers, Jun-Tuk and I will gather the supplies from the snowmobiles. The rest of you are going to set up the tents in here and then tomorrow you will all go home while I continue to try and rescue my wife."

Henry looked over his remaining students with pride for them because of how they had conducted themselves. He smiled at them. "All of you here have performed well beyond what anyone could have asked of you. I am truly honored to have called you my students. I hope that one day you can forgive me for the mistakes that I have made here today." Henry nodded at his students, and then he turned around and walked out of the cave entrance.

CHAPTER 11

The sound of a baby crying continued to echo throughout the cavern as Gina followed the mysterious woman deeper into the cave. Gina was astounded at the length, depth, and width of the cave. There were burning bones of varying lengths that served as torches spread throughout the cave system at irregular intervals. The torches seemed to be embedded in naturally formed crevices that were scattered throughout the cave. From the smell coming from the torches, Gina guessed that the bones were covered in some manner of oil or fat that allowed them to continue burning. Thousands of questions about the cave were running through the young anthropologist's mind. She was about to start asking the native woman about the cave system when a much more obvious question came to her mind.

Gina placed her hand on the native woman's shoulder. "Who are you?

The woman turned around and looked Gina in the eye. "I am Wen-Ku. Like you, I am a wife of the Yeti god. Like you, I am also a caretaker of the young. What shall I call you? You are not from the Quinic tribe. Your clothes and flesh are both strange to me. You are not one of my people." The woman ran her eyes over the beautiful young professor. "I have heard the men of my tribe speak of the people who travel across the ocean in canoes as large as mountains. They say that the mountain canoes come from distant lands to the north." The woman's eyes grew wide. "If you are here, the Yeti god must have traveled over the great ocean to choose you as one of his brides."

Gina smiled politely at the young woman as she thought about the best way to explain her situation to Wen-Ku. "The Yeti is not able to travel across the oceans. I came here on one of the large canoes that you spoke of with other members of my tribe. We were led here by a member of your tribe named Jun-Tuk to learn about your tribe and their ways."

Wen-Ku frowned. "I knew Jun-Tuk when I was younger and his daughter, Shunu. Shunu was brought here as a handmaiden of the

Yeti god not as a bride. She was helping me to care for the young one." At the mention of the young, one Wen-Ku began walking faster. "We must get the young one before his crying alerts the crawling demons to our presence in the cave."

Gina followed Wen-Ku as more questions started to accumulate in her mind. Gina tried to keep track of all of the new questions that she was forming as she spoke to Wen-Ku *Yukon has both brides and handmaidens, what is the distinction between the two sets of women? How long had Wen-Ku been a bride of the Yeti?*

Gina was sweating as she continued to walk through the huge cave. She took off her insulated coat and wrapped it around her waist. The cave was incredibly hot and Gina was sure that the meager torches that lit up part of the cave were not generating the heat that she was feeling. Gina increased the rate at which she was walking so that she was walking next to Wen-Ku. She decided that her best approach to gaining information from Wen-Ku, as well as securing her trust, would be to start by asking Wen-Ku questions that were not associated with Yukon, the women that he had taken, or the baby. By asking questions about the environment, Gina would get a better idea of where she was and what were the potential dangers or benefits that the cave offered to her. Gina was dying to learn more about Yukon, but as an anthropologist, she knew that orienting herself to her environment was the first thing that she needed to do if she hoped to leave the cave alive. Gina pointed farther down the vast cave. "This cave is amazing, I have never seen anything like it. How large is this cave?"

Wen-Ku shook her head. "This is only part of a larger system of tunnels that runs throughout the entire mountain range. The tunnels system is nearly as vast as the valley itself."

Gina was fascinated. "An entire tunnel system that runs throughout the mountain range." She estimated that if the tunnel system ran throughout the entire mountain range that the system must have been hundreds of miles in length. The height and width of the cave was also beyond belief. Yukon was still sleeping near the cave entrance but the twenty-five-foot tall Yeti could easily have walked throughout the majority of the cave.

The deeper that the two women walked into the tunnel, the more Gina could feel the heat in the cave increasing. The heat had reached the point to where Gina was able to take off the majority of her artic gear. She stripped off two layers of clothing so that she was just in her sweat pants and her hooded sweatshirt. She then asked Wen-Ku about the heat. "The cave is so warm. Where does the heat come from?"

Wen-Ku gestured down to the cave floor. "Deep beneath the cave at the base of the mountain lives the great fire god. His hot blood flows throughout the entire tunnel system and warms the inside of the mountains."

Gina nodded as she was fairly certain that Wen-Ku was describing molten lava running throughout the mountain. Wen-Ku words had all but confirmed Gina's suspicions about an underground volcano heating the tunnel system. Gina knew from personal experience that Wen-Ku was provided food by Yukon, but she was not sure about where the native woman obtained her water supply. This was another one of the vital questions that Gina needed to know because staying hydrated was another key factor to her survival. She questioned Wen-Ku again. "After we address the baby, is there anywhere that I can get water? I am extremely thirsty from my long journey here."

Wen-Ku nodded. "The heat created by the great fire god below provides us with water. There are numerous openings to the outside mountain where his heat causes the snow to melt. The water from the melting snow comes down through the openings in the mountains and provides us with fresh water."

As Wen-Ku led Gina farther into the illuminated cavern, she suddenly made a quick left into a side tunnel that served almost as a separate room. There were numerous torches around the room which lit the small cave up as if the sun itself was shining into it. To the far left side of the cave, there was a large crevice in the wall and inside of the crevice there was an infant. Wen-Ku reached into the crevice and pulled the crying infant from within the cave wall. As Gina took a closer look at the infant, she guessed that the baby boy could not have been over a year old. The infant was wrapped in the skin of a mammoth that Yukon must have slain and Wen-Ku then made a blanket out of.

Wen-Ku rocked the infant and calmed the baby down. Wen-Ku then fed the boy and after he was finished Wen-Ku held the baby out to Gina. "This is our son. His name is Thu-Ca."

Gina was again troubled by the way that Wen-Ku had referred to the baby as *our son*. Gina was hesitant to take the child but she did not want to offend Wen-Ku and she still needed a lot of information from the woman. Gina decided that she would need placate the woman for the time being. Gina placed her outer clothing on the floor next to her. She then slowly reached out and accepted the baby in her arms. Gina then sat down and began rocking the baby.

With the babies needs addressed, Gina continued to have Wen-Ku answer all of the questions that were swirling in her mind. She gestured to the torches around the cave. "The baby has more light than the rest of the cave. Does he enjoy the light or does the light serve another purpose?"

Wen-Ku smiled. "I can see that the Yeti god chose well when he picked you to be one of his brides." Wen-Ku pointed to the opening of the cave that they were in. "This cave has only one entrance, and when I am away, I put Thu-Ca into the small crevice that you saw him in. With only a single opening, I try to have as much light as possible near the door. The light will deter the crawling demons from coming to devour the baby."

Gina took note of the fact that Wen-Ku had once again mentioned the crawling demons. After her encounter with the saber-toothed cats and the cave bear, Gina was determined to be aware of us much of the wildlife both in the valley and in the tunnel system as possible. Given the size of the tunnel system, the fact that it was heated, and that it had an ample water supply Gina was sure that it could easily support an entire ecosystem. Gina continued to bounce the baby in her arms as she moved slightly closer to Wen-Ku. "These crawling demons, what are they like?"

A wave of fear ran over Wen-Ku's face. Gina could tell from the woman's expression that whatever the crawling demons were that Wen-Ku was terrified of them and she did not care to talk about them. Wen-Ku took a deep breath to gather her courage. "The crawling demons live deep within the tunnels that run throughout the mountain range. The crawling demons take many forms but there are three forms that are the most dangerous. The first form is that of the many oars. In this form, a crawling demon comes like a long black cloud propelled by hundreds of tiny oars. In this form, the crawling demon will envelope its prey with its body and then devour the prey's head. I saw a crawling demon in this form kill one of the former handmaidens of the Yeti god."

Wen-Ku said a small prayer to the Yeti god at the thought of her fallen friend. She then sighed and continued to inform Gina of the other forms that that the crawling demons could take. "The second form is much larger than the first form. It has a thick hairy black body like that of the great orcas except that it is covered in short fur. In this form, the crawling terror moves on long poles like those made from the bones of the whales that form our tents. In this form, the crawling demon has many eyes that work as one. It often lives in a large net that it will use to trap its prey."

Wen-Ku's body shook as she thought about the third form of the crawling demons. "In the third form, the crawling demon has thick brown fur like the demons that live it the valley. The hair covers the entirety of the demon's body except for its long tail which is naked. In this form, the crawling demon has two long teeth that extend out of its mouth. The demon will use these teeth to tear those that they hunt to pieces. This is the largest form that the crawling demons may take. In this form, the crawling demons are nearly as large as the Yeti god himself."

Gina nodded. "The light. You said that the light will keep them away?"

Wen-Ku shook her head. "No. The crawling demons do not care for the light and they will often shy away from it, but if one of the demons smells an easy meal such as carrion or the baby, they will attack despite the light." Tears began to form in Wen-Ku's eyes and she looked to the floor. "Several moons ago, we lost two of the Yeti god's brides and three of our children to the crawling demons in this form. The light in the room was bright, but the crawling demons were ravenous, and they fought through their fear of the light." Wen-Ku wiped her eyes clear. "When the Yeti god returned to our cave and found that his wives and children had been devoured, he was filled with rage. The Yeti god ran into the tunnels and he hunted down the crawling demons who had slain his family. His vengeance was swift but after the rage had left him his grief lasted for many nights. For the next three moons, he would do nothing but sit by the opening to the cave and howl into the night sky at the pain of the loss of his children." Wen-Ku shook her head. "The light helps to dissuade the crawling demons, but our only true protection from them and from the demons of the valley is the great Yeti god himself."

Gina was gently rocking the baby, and when she looked down at the infant, she noticed that Thu-Ca had fallen asleep. The Quinic woman smiled at Gin. "You will do well as a mother to the children of the Yeti god?"

Gina smiled back at the woman and then she took her opportunity to obtain what information that she could from her. "I hope to be a good mother to the children of the Yeti god but I am stranger to this land. I have no knowledge of the Yeti god and his ways. Nor do I know about his brides or handmaidens. Please tell me what you know of the Yeti's history and how I should conduct myself as one of his brides."

Wen-Ku nodded. "Of course. I shall tell you all that I know so that you may best serve the Yeti god as one of his brides." Wen – Ku closed her eyes. "The Yeti god comes from a tribe of Yeti gods. I have never seen them but some of the brides who were here before me saw them. The Yeti gods have a chief who leads them as they travel with the long-nosed demons they hunt across the great valley. The brides who were here before me say that once long ago the Yeti god that we now worship was once chief of the Yeti's. They say that the Yeti god must have sired many other Yeti gods in his time as ruler of the Yeti tribe. I was told that the Yeti god had ruled his tribe for many years, until one day a younger male Yeti god challenged him as chief of the tribe." Wen-Ku took a deep breath. "The two Yeti's had a mighty battle that shook the mountains and the sky itself. After a long and bloody battle, the younger Yeti god had defeated the old chief. When the old chief had been defeated, he was forced to leave his people. I have been told that he is no longer welcome with them and that is why he stays close to the pass that goes through the mountains and out of the valley."

Gina nodded as she processed this information. The story of Yukon being the leader the tribe, losing a challenge to a younger male, and then being forced to leave the tribe helped to clear up a good deal of questions that Gina had about the Yeti's past. Gina thought about the lives of the gorillas in Africa. She had heard reports that a family of gorillas in Africa was led by an alpha male who in most cases had the breeding rights with all of the females in his group. The alpha male would hold this position of power until another male gorilla challenged his reign. If the younger male won the challenge then he would assume the position of the alpha male and the defeated male would be forced to leave the family and fend for himself. From what Wen-Ku had just said, Gina guessed that Yukon must have been an alpha male who was ousted from his role and was forced to leave his family.

Gina nodded and then continued to question Wen-Ku. "It was after the Yeti god was sent away from his tribe, that he started to come to your tribe, wasn't it?"

Wen-Ku nodded. "Yes, when the Yeti god no longer had his tribe, he started to leave the valley and come to our village. When he first came to our village, his rage was great and he unleashed his mighty power on us. It was not until a young girl offered himself up to him that the Yeti god was finally calmed. She was the first woman from my tribe who the Yeti god had taken." A strange look of pride came over Wen-Ku's face. "She was the first woman to be chosen as one of the Yeti god's brides. The brides, like me, are chosen to live out the rest of our lives caring for the children of the Yeti. The Yeti will also take handmaidens from my village. The handmaidens only stay with us for a few weeks before the Yeti returns them to the Quinic. Prior to their return, the brides have the handmaidens vow to not speak of what occurred to us to the people of our village." Wen-Ku shrugged. "The ways of gods are not meant for humans to know unless a god chooses to give them this knowledge."

Wen-Ku's statement was both confusing and terrifying to Gina because Wen-Ku had referred to Gina as a bride of the Yeti. The anthropologist swallowed hard and she took a hard look at the baby that she was holding. Gina was horrified that Wen-Ku thought of this baby as a child of the Yeti. Gina looked back to

Wen-Ku and then she continued to question the native woman. "Why did you refer to Thu-Ca and the other infants as children of the Yeti?"

Wen-Ku shrugged. "I called him a child of the Yeti because I am his mother and I am the bride of the Yeti god. Since I am the Yeti god's bride, my son is his son."

Gina slowly handed the baby back to Wen-Ku. She then stood up with a look of grave concern on her face. "You said that I was a bride of the Yeti; how do you know that I am bride and not just one of the handmaiden's? How do you know the difference between a bride of the Yeti and a handmaiden?"

Wen-Ku stared at Gina. "The Yeti god gathers handmaidens to help with the brides after the birth of an infant. While the bride recovers from the birth, the handmaidens assist with the child. After the child mother has recovered from giving birth, the Yeti returns the handmaiden to our people. The mother then cares for the child. Thu-Ca is many moons old and I am long recovered from giving birth to him. Also, when the Yeti brings a handmaiden to his cave, he takes her directly to his brides to help care for the children. The great Yeti god did not do this with you. He kept you by him to protect you. You are not a handmaiden; you are a bride."

Gina shook her head in disbelief. "You said that several moons ago you lost some of the brides and the children to the crawling demons, but the Yeti has been taking woman for years. Where are the other mothers and children then? Are they deeper in the tunnels?"

Wen-Ku shrugged. "The crawling demons have devoured them all. Besides you, I am the only current bride and mother left."

Gina's knees became weak and she sank to the floor. Tears were welling up in her eyes as she was counting back days. She then asked the question that she feared would change her life forever. "The Yeti god, how does he determine which women shall be handmaidens and which women shall be his brides?"

Wen-Ku face suddenly filled with joy. "You have not yet discovered it, have you?" She ran over and hugged Gina. "The Yeti god often knows before the brides do, but you are with child!"

Gina burst out crying. This was supposed to be one of the happiest moments in her life. She was supposed to share this news with Henry in the comfort of their home. Her husband should have been holding her in an embrace of joy. She should have been thinking about if she and Henry would find out the sex of the baby. Instead of the vision of happiness that Gina had in her head, she was trapped in a valley of monsters by a Yeti that would never let her go. She had just learned that most babies and their mothers were killed and eaten by the horrors that crawled out of the dark bowels of the Earth. She was in a situation where both she and her baby had been given a death sentence. Gina screamed in anguish at the fate that awaited her and her baby and at the thought that Henry would never know that he was going to be a father.

Wen-Ku stepped back from Gina with a look of confusion on her face. "Why do you weep? Do you not see that Yeti god has lost his family and that he chosen you and your child to be part of his new family? Your child will be the child of a god! If your child reaches adulthood, he will gain the Yeti god's power and rule over the entire valley! If Thu-Ca reaches adult, he and your child shall rule the valley as siblings! We shall be the mothers of the rulers of all that we see!"

When Gina heard what Wen-Ku was saying, she knew that the woman was at least a religious zealot and at the worst she was insane. Instead of causing Gina more distress, this thought helped to focus her. Gina realized that for Henry and for the sake of her unborn child that she needed to escape the Yeti and valley. She also realized that if she was going to get away from the Yeti and out of the valley that she would have to placate both Yukon and Wen-Ku.

Gina forced herself to stop crying and then she stood up and hugged Wen-Ku. "My weeping is because I am overwhelmed with joy! As you said, my child shall be the child of a god!" Gina walked over to her coat and switched on the beacon that was in her pocket. She sighed when she saw that the beacon was on but not transmitting. She smiled at Wen-Ku. "Come with me, I wish to walk back to the Yeti god. We should stay close to him for protection, should we not? The crawling demons devoured the other brides and their children. We would not want the same fate to befall us and our babies, would we?"

Wen-Ku nodded and pulled Thu-Ca close her breast. "You are correct. The Yeti god is our only protection. Let us go and sit with him while he sleeps."

Gina walked next to Wen-Ku as they navigated their way back through the tunnels. Gina knew that if she was able to get close enough to the cave opening that transmitter would work. She hoped that if she was out in the open that her radio may even work as well. Still, Gina knew that if a rescue team was to mount an expedition that even if they were to find her that Yukon would kill everyone who tried to rescue her. Gina would turn the transmitter on so that the team could start the long journey to her but she knew that she would have to escape from Yukon before she could rendezvous with anyone. Gina began reviewing all of the information that she had gathered from Wen-Ku, and as she did so, an escape plan was quickly forming in her mind.

CHAPTER 12

Henry said a small prayer as he threw the cold snow over two more of the deceased graduate students. Gordon had pointed out that they needed to bury or burn the bodies of both the rescue team members and the teratorns in order to prevent attracting more of the ravenous giant birds. Henry had taken the coat from the dead student that he was burying. The student would not need the coat anymore, and with the tear in Henry's coat, he would face freezing to death in the quickly approaching night. Henry did a quick count in his head. His rescue party had shrunken from a team of twenty-four people to a team of sixteen. They had only been in the valley for a few hours and they had already lost a third of the team. Henry felt like mentally scolding himself for losing the lives of the team members. He took a deep breath and reminded himself that he still had sixteen other people who he needed to get out of this valley alive. He knew full well that cursing and doubting himself would do nothing to help him reach the goal of getting the rest of the team out alive. With that in mind, he pushed the self-blame to the back of his mind and focused on what the next step was in getting the rest of the team members home safely.

Henry looked around to see Gordon finishing up burying one of the teratorns. To Gordon's left, Rodgers was using his hunting knife to slice the head off one of the dead teratorns. Henry had no doubt that Rodgers would try to take the head home, have it stuffed, and take full credit for killing the monster himself. Rodgers had finished his grizzly task just as the sun started to set over the mountains. Rodgers took a moment to point at the decapitated teratorn. "This dammed bird's feathers are far thicker than I thought they would be." The hunter shrugged. "Thick feathers must be some sort of adaptation they have made in order to survive in the cold down here."

Gordon gestured the other two men to head back to cave. Rodgers picked up the teratorn head and followed Gordon back up to the slope to the cave. When they had entered the large cave, Henry was pleased to see that the remaining team members had set up over a dozen insulated tents. The cave was large enough that all of the tents were able to be spaced along its floor with room to spare. Henry had not taken the time to notice before when the teratorns were attacking but the cave seemed to have no end. Henry wondered how far the cave went into the mountain but he quickly pushed the thought aside rationalizing that now was not the time to go on a spelunking trip.

Gordon called over Henry, Rodgers, and Dana. When they were all gathered in a tight circle, Gordon reviewed their current status with them. "Eight people in all have died today. We have already used up more than half of the ammunition that we brought into the valley. We only have about sixty rounds left for the rifles. We are also facing the prospect that most of our snowmobiles have already used up roughly half of their gas supply. We can siphon the gasoline from the two snowmobiles whose riders were killed in the teratorn attack." He looked to Henry. "If you still want to pursue your wife, we can put the gasoline from one of the snowmobiles into your vehicle and then disperse the rest between the remaining snowmobiles. With more gas, we can travel at top speed all the way out of the valley. When we reach the camp, I will start having people evacuate back to the ship where they are safe."

Henry nodded. "Okay, that sounds like a plan. I have already spoken to Jun-Tuk. He wishes to accompany me in an attempt to rescue Gina. He says that he still needs proof that the Yeti is not a god in order to keep more of his people from giving themselves up to this creature." He looked toward Rodgers. "Can you leave him your crossbow? He says that he knows how to use it and it would be helpful to not have him totally defenseless out there." Rodgers nodded in affirmation of Henry's request.

Dana shrugged. "What difference will that make? The people should continue to give up one girl every couple of months to the Yeti. We have seen what he will do if he wants something and he is denied access to it. If he is not given a girl, he could very well destroy their entire village. They don't have any weapon even close to powerful enough to stop the Yeti."

Henry nodded. "That's true. The Quinic do not have any weapons capable of hurting the Yeti, but we do." He looked at

Gordon. "We have some dynamite back at our home base that is used to move large areas of rock if we need to. When you get back to camp, have the demolition experts place the dynamite on either side of the valley pass. Two days from now, whether or not Gina or I return from the valley, blow the sides of the mountain that make up the valley pass. It will cause a landslide that not even that dammed Yeti will be able to dig through. Jun-Tuk's people will be free of the Yeti. Hopefully, Gina and I are back by then, but if we are not, get the demolition guys aboard ship and head home." He looked in everyone's eyes. "Are we all in agreement with the plan?"

Rodgers shook his head. "You need to split that gasoline up three ways between Henry's snowmobile, the team, and one more snowmobile because I am going after the Yeti with you."

Henry looked at the man in surprise. "Rodgers, you don't have to that for us. You will still get paid for going on the expedition. Gordon has written instructions from me for the Board of Directors at Princeton. They will pay everyone in full when the ship returns to the States."

Rodgers sneered. "I don't really give a damn about you, your wife, or your pay. I am a hunter and the greatest game in the history of mankind is out there in that Yeti. I am not leaving this place without his head." Rodgers could see the anger swelling in Henry's face. The hunter smiled. "Look Henry, you don't need to like me or approve of my reasons for going forward but you know that both you and your wife stand a better chance of getting out of here alive if I go with you after the monster."

Henry nodded. "Okay, let's get some sleep. We will all head out first thing tomorrow morning. Don't even worry about breaking down the tents. Just head for the valley pass and get out of this hellish place. If the rest of us are still alive to try and make it back to you, leaving the tents up will leave us a place that we can stop overnight if we need to."

Gordon nodded and they all went their separate ways. Dana, Henry, and Gordon all walked to their tents but Rodgers picked up his teratorn head and walked toward the back of the cave past the last of the tents. When he was clear of the tents, he tossed the head a little farther in to the cave. "Alright my lovely, you just stay safe and sound there until I come back for you in a few days." Rodgers then turned and headed for his tent even as the stench of the decapitated bird wafted farther into the cave. Deep inside of the cave system, two large black forms started moving toward the mouth of the cave when the smell of the dead teratorn reached them.

An hour after they had retired to their tents, Dana Summers was still rolling back and forth wide awake. The horrible images of the events that had occurred over the past twenty four hours were still replaying themselves in her head. She knew that that those same events could repeat themselves tomorrow. She knew that there was good possibility that she and everyone else was going to be die before they made it out of the valley. She rolled over one more time and then said aloud, "The hell with it." She unzipped her tent and walked out into the miniature tent city that had been formed in the cave. She quietly crept between the tents until she came to Gordon's tent. She stopped in front of his tent and whispered, "Tony, it's Dana. I need to talk to you." Gordon unzipped his tent and Dana quickly rushed into it. She threw herself on top of Gordon and she passionately kissed the young hunter.

Dana pulled away from Gordon and then she started talking to him at a frantic pace, "Look, I don't know what this is and I barely know what I am doing. If want me to leave, just point and I will go back to my tent. I just keep thinking about those kids that died out there today and all of the things that they will never get the chance to do. My chance taking days may be over tomorrow for all that I know so I thought that I would take a chance right now." Gordon was a silent as ever as he stared at the attractive doctor.

When he didn't respond, Dana stood up. "I'm sorry. I'll just head back to my tent."

Gordon grabbed her arm. "Please don't go. I wanted to take a chance too. I just didn't think that an educated woman who saves lives for a living would see much of a future with a professional killer like me."

Dana leaned in closer to Gordon. "In this valley, there is no future. There is only right now. Right now is all that we have and all that we may ever have." She kissed him again and then pulled away. She started taking off her coat and her shirt. "So right now, let's make the most of our time together."

Gordon grabbed her hand to keep her from taking her shirt off. "Don't. Even with the extra heat in the cave, it is far too cold for you to have no clothes on."

She leaned forward and kissed him again. "In sub-zero survival situations, the best way to keep warm is to wrap yourself naked in a blanket with someone else who is also naked. That way you share body heat." She smiled at Gordon. "Trust me, I am a doctor." Dana kissed Gordon again and then she started pulling his shirt off. When they had both relieved each other of their clothing, they pulled a thick blanket over themselves and they made the most of the present.

It was just before sunrise when Henry was awakened by a blood-curdling scream that came from the back of the cave where the last tent was positioned. Henry grabbed his flashlight and rifle then he sprang out of his tent. He ran to the back of the cave with the flashlight's beam of light bouncing off the cave walls. When he reached the back of the cave, he unleashed his own scream of terror. He saw a colossal black shape wiggling through a hole in the tent that was farthest back in the cave. A second later, the black shape pulled its body back out of the hole in the tent with the head of one of the female team members in its mouth. Henry screamed and fired at the giant insect. "Gordon, Rodgers, get out here! Everyone else, wake up and make for the front of the cave!"

The giant millipede's body jerked from side to side as Henry continued to fire on the wretched creature. Henry had to literally blow the colossal insect's head off to finally kill it. Henry was just about to breathe a sigh of relief when three more of the huge millipedes came crawling out from the back of the cave. One of the wretched creatures was chewing on the teratorn head that Rodgers had thrown deep into the cave. Henry cursed Rodgers then he started firing at the millipedes.

Rodgers walked out of his tent with his rifle in hand, to see Dana Summers running out of Gordon's tent. Gordon exited his tent right behind Dana with his rifle in his hands. Rodgers laughed. "Well Gordon, it seems as if I will have to admit that you bagged the best prize on this hunting trip!"

Gordon ignored Rodgers and ran next to Henry where the two of them quickly finished off the three millipedes that had made their way to the tents. Henry turned his flashlight deeper in the cave to see a half dozen more giant millipedes crawling toward them. Henry turned to Gordon, "The teratorn head that the Rodgers threw back there drew them in." He then looked over his shoulder at the cave opening. "There is no way those cold-blooded insects can live in the polar temperatures out there. It must be the heat in the caves that allows them to thrive in here." Henry put his rifle over his shoulder. "We are just wasting bullets in here; we need to get outside as quickly as possible."

Henry could see the remaining team members rushing out into the sub-zero temperatures outside of the cave. He caught site of Dana grabbing the radio, and the receiver that they needed to track Gina. The young doctor also grabbed a handful of flares and an emergency first aid kit before she ran out of the cave. Henry looked back at the approaching millipedes. He thought that along with Gordon and Rodgers, that he would be able to cover everyone from the advancing millipedes. He realized how wrong he was when he saw the thick black form of a giant millipede drop from the ceiling and onto one of the fleeing rescue team members. The man screamed as the millipede's pincer cracked his skull open like an egg. Henry forgot that he was fighting with insects that could defy gravity and cling to walls and ceilings. He shined his light onto the cave ceiling to find that it was covered with giant millipedes.

Henry and Gordon ran toward the cave entrance as two more millipedes dropped down on top of two graduate students just before they reached the safety of the cold temperatures. Henry tried to target one of the millipedes that had dropped onto one of his student's, but before he could aim his rifle, the massive insect had crushed the young man's skull.

Henry started once more running for the cave entrance when another millipede dropped directly in front of Gordon. The insect lifted the front half of its body off the cave floor and the burly hunter took the opportunity to kick the insect in its underbelly. Gordon then used his rifle like a club to strike the insect across its face. With the insect reeling, Henry took aim and fired two bullets into the millipede's head, turning it into a pulpy goo. A millipede dropped behind Henry and Gordon returned the favor by slaying the insect before it could attack Henry.

Dana was at the front of the cave screaming, "Tony, Henry, everyone who is still alive is clear! Get the hell out of there!"

Gordon and Henry sprinted to the cave entrance as countless giant millipedes fell to the cave floor behind them. The giant insects were closing in on them quickly. They had almost reached the two men when out of desperation Dana Summers pulled a flare from her pocket, lit it, and threw it at the attacking millipedes. When the bright burning flare landed in front of the millipede horde, the grotesque creatures recoiled at the bright burning light. The millipedes began to make a strange hissing sound at the flare and then most of the insects started to recede into the darkness and warmth of the cave.

Henry and Gordon had continued to run as the millipedes were slowly retreating behind them. They were only a step away from exiting the cave when a millipede dropped from the ceiling and blocked the entrance. The monstrous creature reared up to its full fifteen foot height and hissed at the two men. They could hear Dana scream from the outside of the cave and then an arrow burst out of the front of the millipede's head. The creature writhed uncontrollably in pain as it tried to remove the arrow that stuck out of both sides of its head. Henry looked around the creature to see Jun-Tuk loading another arrow into Rodger's crossbow. Henry then shared a quick glance with Gordon. The two men nodded at each other then they both lowered their shoulders and charged the writhing horror. Like a pair of professional tag team wrestlers, they stuck the giant millipede in unison and sent the pitch black insect tumbling out into the freezing valley. As the insect slide down the snowy mountain side, Henry and Gordon ran out into the cold as an army of millipedes stopped just short of the cave entrance.

To the left of the two men was the dying insect that they had pushed out of the cave. Henry and Gordon walked carefully around the quickly freezing millipede as it tried in vain to make its way through the ice and snow. When they reached the bottom of the hill, Dana ran over and hugged Gordon. Rodgers laughed, but a quick look from the muscular Gordon quickly quieted the portly hunter.

Henry took a quick count of how many people had made it out of the cave alive. Aside from himself, Gordon, Dana, Rodgers, and Jun-Tuk, only five members of the original team were still alive. Henry didn't waste any more time. He simply started shouting out orders, "Gordon, we now have plenty of gasoline." He pointed to two snowmobiles to his left. "Siphon what you can from those two snowmobiles. Then fill up the other snowmobiles as much as you can. When the snowmobiles that you are siphoning from are empty, flip them on their sides." Henry pointed to two more snowmobiles to the right. "Leave those three vehicles up right. If we are in a hurry when we are coming back this way, at least we will know that all we need to do is make it to those vehicles. If we need to switch snowmobiles, we will have enough gas to make it back home." He walked over closer to Gordon. "Remember, two days from now, blow that valley pass and make sure that the Yeti and none of these other dammed monsters ever get out of this valley again."

Gordon simply nodded then he started setting up the siphon to fill up the gas tanks. Henry next walked over to Rodgers. "Make sure that each group has plenty of ammunition and flares. We already know that the Yeti will stop into the caves from the tracks that we followed here. There is a good chance that we will not only run into Yeti in those caves, but the millipedes as well. If we do, having the flares around may be even a better solution than the using the rifles."

CHAPTER 13

Wen-Ku was carrying the now awake and cooing Thu-ca in her arms as she led Gina back to the mouth of the cave. When the women reached the cave opening, they found that Yukon was wide awake. The Yeti was staring out at the snow and snarling at something. Gina had taken her time to put her winter clothing back on and she approached the Yeti while Wen-Ku stayed farther back in the warmer recesses of the cave. Gina walked up next to the Yeti and she looked out to see two gigantic birds of prey tearing apart the remains of the cave bear that Yukon had slain earlier.

From the look of the huge birds, Gina guessed that they were some form of teratorn. As an anthropologist, Gina was well aware that teratorns had fed on man and other primates when our ancestors first made their way out of the trees. From the way that Yukon was acting, she guessed that the Yeti still saw the birds as an annoyance if not an outright threat. The teratorns were large but not nearly as tall as Yukon. Gina guessed that the birds would have weighed less than a quarter of what the Yeti did. Most birds of prey did not attack prey larger than themselves, and even though she doubted it, Gina could not say for sure that the teratorns would not attempt to prey on Yukon. Gina also considered the fact that these animals did live in a polar environment. It was entirely possible that the normal fear of attacking something larger and heavier than oneself may be negated by the overall scarcity of food. It then dawned on Gina, that aside from being a threat to Yukon himself, the teratorns may have been a threat to infant Yeti's or to the women and human infants that Yukon tried to surround himself with.

Gina walked to the edge of the cave, and the transmitter in her pocket blinked. A rush of hope coursed through Gina's body. The transmitter was working and it would be able to lead a rescue team to her. When Gina thought that her life was the only one in danger, she didn't want anyone else risking their lives to save her. Now that she knew she was going to be mother her entire perspective had changed. She felt the need to do anything that she could to protect her unborn child. The people who yesterday she did not want risking their lives for her she now prayed would challenge the dangers of the valley to rescue her baby.

Gina was still thinking of her saving her unborn child when Yukon suddenly growled and stood. Gina looked out of the cave to see the two teratorns squawking. The two birds looked to the left of the cave and then they took the air. Yukon walked to edge of the cave and Gina followed closely behind the Yeti. Yukon took a step out of the cave and Gina peered around the huge Yeti to see what she at first thought was another cave bear lumbering along the side of the mountain. The movements of the animal seemed much more labored and clumsy than the way the bear moved. As Gina looked slightly closer at the approaching beast, she could see that the creature was not a bear. The creature stopped along the mountain side and started digging into the snow. A second later, Gina saw a long thin tongue reach out and lick the area that the beast had just dug up. When she saw the long tongue, it reminded Gina of the sloths that she had seen at various zoos. Gina decided that the large animal must have been a giant ground sloth. She also deduced that most of the vegetation found in the valley must have grown along the slopes of the mountains where the heat from the volcano below could keep mosses and short grasses from totally freezing to death.

There was a loud squawk and Gina looked above the giant sloth to see the two teratorns circling the animal. One of the horrible birds swooped down and attacked the giant sloth. The other teratorn followed the lead of its partner and attacked the sloth as well. Gina shrugged and spoke to herself, "Well, I guess that answers my question if the teratorns would attack something larger than themselves or not."

Gina watched as the giant sloth stood on its hind legs and started rolling its huge paws in front of itself like a heavyweight boxer. The teratorns continued to fly around the beast while using their beaks and claws to attack it. Spurts of blood flew into the air as the teratorns scratched and pecked at the giant sloth. The sloth continued to try and defend himself by striking the teratorns with its huge paws. Gina was impressed that the sloth continued to step forward as he threw his punches. Gina's MMA training had taught her that stepping forward when you punched helped to put your weight behind a blow. In the case of a giant sloth that weighed over a ton, putting his weight into a blow gave him a lot of punching power.

The two teratorns continued to circle the sloth and attack it for several seconds before the sloth was able to land a blow on one of the wretched birds. When the sloth's blow connected with the bird's chest, its entire body bent in half. Gina was sure that the sloth's blow had shattered the teratorn's ribcage and crushed its heart. Despite the death of its partner, the first teratorn continued to try and attack the sloth. The teratorn continued to circle the sloth and it was obvious to Gina that the raptor was trying to attack the creature's face and eyes. While attacking the sloth's vulnerable face was the only chance of success that the teratorn had, it also placed the bird directly in the range of the sloth's paws. The teratorn continued to attack in a blur of feathers until the sloth punched the bird in its chest and crushed its skeleton just as it had the other teratorn. With his attackers defeated, the sloth slumped back down onto all fours and started digging in the snow again.

The poor animal thought that it was safe until Yukon leapt out of the cave and sprinted toward the sloth. Gina stepped farther out of the cave to watch Yukon's attack on the giant sloth. She was still trying to learn as much about the Yeti as possible, not only for posterities' sake, but also to increase her own chances of escaping the monster. When the giant sloth saw Yukon running toward it, the beast's eyes grew wide with fear. Gina could almost feel the sloth's terror at the sight of the Yeti. From the look on the animal's face, Gina could see that the sloth saw Yukon as death incarnate. The giant sloth once again stood up on its hind legs and began rolling its massive paws in front of itself.

When the sloth stood up, Yukon stopped running and he began to walk toward his prey. When Yukon was just out of the reach of the sloth's paws, he stopped walking and stared at the animal. Gina could already see how this encounter was going to play itself out. Aside from training in mixed martial arts, Gina was an avid fan of the UFC. She remembered a highly publicized fight in which multiple time heavyweight boxing champion James Toney had taken on several time UFC champion Randy Couture. When the match had started, Toney and Couture were sizing each other up in exactly the same fashion that the giant sloth and Yukon were now. When she was watching the fight on television, she knew that Toney only had one chance of winning the fight. Toney had undeniable knockout power and all he had to do was hit Couture once to knockout the MMA fighter. The danger for Toney was that if he missed with his first punch, Couture's superior speed and grappling techniques would allow him to get inside of Toney's defenses and then tear the boxer apart.

Gina knew that just like James Toney the giant sloth had one shot. Yukon was a powerful beast but from what she had read about giant sloths and from what she had seen in his battle with teratorns Gina was sure that one well-placed punch from the sloth could crush Yukon's skull. When Yukon had battled the saber-toothed cats and the cave bear, Gina had prayed the Yeti would defeat the beasts and save her from being devoured. Now that she knew Yukon intended to keep her and her child captive for the rest of their lives, she prayed that the giant sloth would kill the Yeti. With Yukon dead, she thought that there was a chance that she could just wait in the cave until a heavily armed rescue team made its way to her and took her out of this hellish valley.

Gina watched with baited breath, as Yukon slowly started to circle to the sloth's left hand side. The clumsy sloth tried to turn with Yukon but it was obvious that the awkward creature was not designed to have much mobility when it was standing on two feet. Yukon continued to slowly circle the sloth until the sloth's feet slid slightly off balance. With the sloth off balance, Yukon charged. The sloth threw a wild blow. Then, in what looked like a replay of the Toney-Couture fight, the nimble Yukon ducked under the blown. The Yeti wrapped his arms around the sloth's waste then he drove the sloth into the ground. The sloth's entire body was jarred by the impact, and while it was still stunned, Yukon mounted the beast's chest. In a flash, Yukon lifted his claw into the air and slashed open the giant sloth's throat. The dying animal shook its head from side to side in agony until Yukon sank his jaws into what was left of the sloth's neck. With one pull, Yukon tore out the sloth's windpipe. The sloth's body shook violently for a few seconds and then the huge animal died. Yukon roared then the blood-soaked Yeti started to devour his kill.

Gina was so enthralled by the battle that she had not noticed Wen-Ku standing next to her at the cave mouth. The native woman smiled when she saw Yukon tearing apart his kill. "The Yeti god has provided us with a sloth. We shall eat well tonight and his body shall provide much for us. His skin will make fine clothing and blankets, his insides shall provide us with fire, and we can turn his bones into many torches." Wen-Ku nodded. "Yes, soon we shall eat well and then we will have much work to do." The native woman turned and walked back into the cave. Gina watched her briefly to see where she had put the baby. Gina watched as Wen-Ku walked over to another unseen crevice that she pulled the baby out of.

Gina took a moment to consider all that she had learned in the past several minutes. First and foremost, she had learned that it looked like most of the vegetation in the valley grew on the mountain slopes. This also meant that most of the animals probably stayed close to the slopes because herbivores stayed near vegetation and carnivores stayed near herbivores. That meant that if Gina tried to escape that it would be safer for her to head for the center of the valley and away from the slopes because she would be less likely to run into any animals. Still, she knew that trying to escape was a futile effort unless Yukon was dead or otherwise engaged.

She had also learned what the primary materials were that Wen-Ku had used to create fire. She would soon also have the opportunity to watch the process through which Wen-Ku obtained these materials from the dead sloth. Lastly, she had learned that cave system seemed to have numerous crevices that were capable of hiding and infant. Gina looked at the cave wall and she wondered if there were crevices along it that were capable of hiding a full-grown woman.

Wen-Ku had said that the crawling demons lived deeper within the tunnel system and that they would be drawn to dead meat. Gina took one more look outside of the cave at Yukon tearing apart the dead sloth. She stared at the dead sloth because in it she saw the key to enacting her desperate escape plan.

Gina waited patiently at the mouth of the cave, as Yukon devoured most of the remains from the dead sloth. While Yukon was eating, Gina had tried to use her radio to contact Dana or anyone else on the radio. She tried multiple channels but all that she could get was static. Gina guessed that the cave and the mountains around her were wreaking havoc on the radio signal and bouncing it all over the place. She put the radio back into her pocket and looked over at the transmitter that she had left just outside of the cave entrance. She was glad to see that beacon on it was still blinking red. She hoped that the blinking light meant that the signal being bounced off the satellite was still reaching the receiver back at camp.

A few feet behind Gina, Wen-Ku was building a fire. Gina watched as the native woman first placed the sleeping Thu-Ca into a cave crevice then gathered dung that Yukon had left around the cave to fuel the fire with. When she had enough dung piled together, Wen-Ku went over to one of the torches that was burning low. She pulled the bone torch out of the crevice that it had been wedged into then she walked over and set the dung pile on fire.

Wen-Ku held the torch out in front of her as it flickered out. She pointed to the torch. "The fat of the last animal that I used to light the torches has nearly all burned away. The lights will begin to dim soon. As soon as we finish eating, we must remove the sloth's fat in order relight the torches lest the crawling demons should return." Wen-Ku grabbed one of the long pelts that she had left sitting near the cave entrance. She threw it on her shoulders then she looked at Gina. "When the Yeti god has finished eating, he will bring a large portion of meat to the cave for us. You watch over the infant and cook the meat; I shall go over to the carcass and remove as much fat from it as I can."

Gina shook her head. "No, I do not know how to cook sloth but I do know the difference between lean meat and fat. You should cook the meat. I shall cut the fat from the dead sloth."

Wen-Ku shrugged. "As you wish." She then looked around the cave floor for a moment, picked up a jagged rock, and handed it to Gina. "Use this to cut the fat from the carcass but be quick about. It will not be long before more of the flying black demons return to feast upon the kill. If they came across you outside of the cave, they shall attack you as well."

Gina nodded in reply and then she took the jagged rock from Wen-Ku just as Yukon had finished his meal. She looked out into the valley to see the blood-soaked form of Yukon walking back toward the cave entrance with a large chunk of sloth meat in his hand. Blood dripped from the chunk of sloth as Yukon made his way into the cave. The Yeti threw the meat down by the fire. He then walked away from the burning flames and over to the crevice where Thu-Ca was sleeping. The blood-soaked monster looked in at the sleeping infant, and as he did so, Gina could see a genuine look of caring on Yukon's face. While Gina was surprised that a monster who could be so brutal could also appear as loving as the Yeti now did, the sight also disgusted her even more as she thought about the monster staring into a crevice at her child.

Yukon lay down next to the crevice and Gina was actually thankful that the Yeti had done so. She was about to put her plan into action and she was afraid that when her plan came together that she would be placing the innocent child in danger. The only thing that she could do to keep the infant safe was to have him as close Yukon as possible. To have Yukon sleeping in front of the baby was about as close to the infant as he could get.

Gina walked out in the subzero temperatures of the valley. She ran over to the dead sloth then she began cutting large strips of fat off of the carcass. Gina had not had to dissect anything since her days in college. She had almost forgotten how horrible the insides of a recently dead creature could smell. She thought Han Solo cutting up the Taun-Taun in *The Empire Strikes Back,* and for the first time since she had entered the valley, she laughed.

After she had cut off several strips of fat, she also cut off several hunks of meat and stuffed them into her pockets. The meat was wet and Gina had to push it deep into her pocket to prevent Wen-Ku from seeing it when she walked back into the cave. With her task complete, Gina turned and walked back up to the cave. When she entered the cave, she saw that Wen-Ku had placed two large stones on either side of the fire. There was a long flat stone that was balanced on the two large stones over the fire.

Wen-Ku was holding two ribs over the flames and she pointed at the flat stone. "Place the fat on the stone over the flames. The heat will melt the fat and make it like water." Gina threw the strips of fat on the fire. She then looked into the cavern at the dying torches. "I will take a look the torches and see what ones we need to replace first. "

Wen-Ku nodded. "Yes, that would be wise. Be careful, though; as the light dies, the crawling demons will make their way closer to the cave opening."

Gina nodded then she began walking deeper into the cave. As she walked through the endless cave, the dying torches flickered and cast ominous shadows onto the wall. As Gina looked at the dancing shadows, her heart began to pound so fast that it hurt her chest. Gina still didn't know what exactly the crawling demons that Wen-Ku had described were. All that she knew about the crawling demons was that they had killed all of Yukon's other brides, they shied away from light, they were drawn in by the smell of dead animals, and that Yukon was the only thing capable of protecting her from them. As she walked farther away from Yukon and deeper into the dying light of the inner cave with pockets full of dead sloth meat, she knew that she had all but turned on a neon sign calling for the crawling demons to attack her.

Gina heard a noise ahead of her and she stopped dead in her tracks. Every survival instinct in her body told her to turn around and run back to Yukon. She had almost turned around when she felt a twinge in her stomach. She knew that it was only her nerves reacting to the situation that she was in, but it reminded her that she needed to escape the Yeti for something more than herself. Gina reminded herself that she knew this plan was dangerous when she had conceived it but it seemed to be her only hope. If she was to turn around and run back to Yukon, she did not know when she would have another chance to contrive a situation that would allow her to escape. She also knew that this was her best option at engaging Yukon to the point that she could make her way out into the middle of the valley. Gina knew that if she ran back to Yukon that she was dooming herself and her unborn child to a short life of terror followed by death. She thought better to spare both herself and the child of that torture and either escape or to die trying now. She told herself that the sound she had heard was just the wind making its way through the caves and she prayed that her assumption was accurate.

Gina grabbed a dying torch off the wall then she walked deeper into the cave, well out of the sight of Wen-Ku. When Gina was sure that the native woman could not see her, she started pulling the sloth meat out of her pockets and stuffing it into the crevices in the walls. After she had stuffed all of the meat into the walls, she quickly hurried back to the mouth of the cave.

When Gina had made her way to front of the cave, she saw Wen-Ku standing next to Yukon. The woman held the charred remains of the sloth rib that she had eaten in her hand. Wen-Ku smiled at her, tossed the meatless bone aside, then the native woman curled up next to Yukon. Despite the fact that Wen-Ku had seen numerous other brides and their children devoured by the animals in the valley and the horrors in the tunnels, she still felt as if she privileged to be the bride of a god. Had Gina not been trapped with the woman, the anthropologist in her would have been fascinated by the Wen-Ku's thought process. Gina would have studied how Wen-Ku perceived her own and her son's relationship with what they considered to be a god. The fact that Gina felt nothing but contempt for a woman who was so proud to keep her child in circumstances that assured him a quick and horrible death confirmed for Gina that she was no longer an anthropologist. She was a woman and a mother who wanted to save the lives of herself and her child. She peered into the crevice in which Thu-Ca was sleeping and her heart sank as the realization that she was also a human being set in on her. Gina knew that Wen-Ku would never willingly leave Yukon. Wen-Ku would also never allow her son or as she had said *the Yeti god's child* to leave the cave either. The native women would die in this cave one way or the other, and so would her son. Wen-Ku's beliefs were in direct opposition with the Gina's beliefs. Gina took a deep breath and thought of a time in the future when she was home and far away from the horror that she was in now. She thought about telling Henry that she had left a child to die in the Yeti's cave. She thought about one day telling her own child that she had saved from the valley about how she had left another child to be devoured by the creatures that lived there. Most of all, she thought about seeing her reflection in the mirror every day and knowing that she had left an infant in a living hell and that she didn't do anything to try and save the infant. Tears began to form in her eyes as she resolved herself to the act of kidnapping an infant from its mother.

Gina wiped her eyes clean and she spoke to herself in English, "It's the lesser of two evils and it what's better for the baby." She sobbed. "It's also the only way that I will be able to live with myself if I get out of here alive." She walked over the mouth of the cave, picked up a second charred sloth rib, and forced herself to take a few bites of it. The meat tasted horrible but Gina knew that she needed some food in her stomach if she had any hope of seeing her escape plan succeed. She tried to be thankful that unlike her last meal that at least the meat she was eating now was cooked. When Gina was finished eating, she tossed the rib outside of the cave. Then she grabbed one of the pelts that Wen-Ku had left there. She wrapped the pelt around herself as she walked back to Yukon and laid down as close to the Yeti as she possibly could. Her entire body shook from a mixture of fear and anticipation. She reviewed the remainder of her plan aloud in English, "Now to just wait for whatever the crawling demons are to come out of the tunnels. When Yukon attacks them, I just have to grab the baby, wrap the pelt around him, run out of the cave, grab the transmitter, and head for the center of the valley." She said, "Just survive all of that and then hope that the rescue team is not too far off before something else attacks me."

CHAPTER 14

Henry had Jun-Tuk with him as he was driving his snowmobile alongside the Yeti tracks at the base of the mountain. Rodgers was following in his own snowmobile only a few feet behind them. Henry's thoughts were scattered between the deaths of his team members and the concern that he still felt over Gina. His concentration was brought to the present when Jun- Tuk tapped on his shoulder.

The old man pointed to Henry's coat pocket. "Your coat, it glows like the sun itself and then disappears only to return again."

Henry looked down at his coat to see an orange light blinking in his pocket. He pulled his snowmobile to a stop then he reached into his pocket to pull out the distress receiver. The receiver was not only blinking, but it was displaying coordinates. Henry's heart leapt for joy at the sight of the blinking receiver because it meant that Gina had turned the transmitter on. As of this very instant, Henry knew that Gina was still alive.

Rodgers pulled to a stop beside Henry. "What are we stopping for? The tracks continue this way and I sure as hell don't want to spend another night in this valley!"

Henry held out the receiver for Rodgers to see. "The transmitter! Gina must have turned it on! That means that she is alive!" Jun-Tuk could see that Henry was overjoyed and he asked Henry what the significance of the blinking light was. Henry translated the implications of what the receiver meant and the old man hugged Henry in a show of his mutual joy.

Rodgers felt a rush of excitement run through his body as well. The hunter was not overjoyed that Gina Murella was seemingly alive. Rodgers' entire body was shaking with anticipation at the prospect of being the first person in history to kill a Yeti. Rodgers pointed to the receiver. "How far away is the transmitter from us right now?"

Henry read the information pouring through the receiver, and as he was reading it, a large smile appeared on his face. He looked up from the receiver. "It looks like she is only about three quarters of a mile from where we are right now! We are almost there! We almost have Gina back!"

It was now Rodgers who was smiling as he looked at Henry. "Not just almost to Gina. We are also just about fifteen minutes away from taking on the single greatest creature that is walking the face of the Earth."

The joy suddenly rushed out of Henry's face. "The Yeti. It took most of our ammunition to kill those teratorns and we weren't even able to slow down the woolly rhino. The Yeti tore apart a mammoth with his bare hands. How are we going to kill a monster that strong?"

Rodgers smiled. "That's easy. We are going to shoot the damned thing right through its eye. There is not a creature on the planet that a well-placed bullet to eye won't hurt. At the very least, we will blind the creature, and at best, the bullet will go right into its brain and kill the thing with one shot."

Henry stared at Rodgers with a skeptical look on his face. "Are you sure that you can hit that Yeti in the eye with your first shot? If his bones are anywhere near as thick as those of the wooly rhino, a shot that hits him in the head may just bounce off his skull and do nothing more than enrage him."

Rodgers nodded. "Don't worry, I can hit that monster in the eye."

Henry was still skeptical about the hunter's ability to shoot the Yeti in the eye before the monster was upon them, but at the same time, he didn't have a better plan. Henry nodded. "Alright, let's keep heading forward."

The group continued on for another ten minutes until they saw several large brown and black forms standing over two blood-soaked forms at the base of the mountain. Henry and Rodgers pulled out their binoculars. Henry gasped when he saw what the large brown and black forms were. Henry's mind was flooded with the fairy tales that he had heard as a kid. Fairy tales like Little Red Riding Hood and the Three Little Pigs. In those stories, wolves had been over exaggerated in terms of their size, cunning, and ferocity. Those fairy tales had been told to scare children so that they respected the wilderness outside of their doors and the potential dangers that lurked in the woods. The wolves in those stories were only allegories for the highwaymen who were the true dangers to young children in the woods. In most cases, wolves presented very little danger to humans. For the most part, wolves were scared of humans, but as Henry stared at these wolves, he knew that these creatures would think nothing of attacking a human. These wolves were the size of Clydesdale Horses and their teeth were larger than a lion's. As Henry looked at the massive wolves, he immediately knew that they were some evolutionary offshoot of the deadly dire wolf. Seeing the killing machines ahead of him touched a primal fear deep within Henry. He looked over at Rodgers and Jun-Tuk and he wondered if they would be all that different from the three little pigs in the eyes of the dire wolves.

Rodgers finally spoke to Henry, "Those giant wolves look to be eating something that I would guess used to be some kind of large cat." Rodgers pointed to several tracks in the snow around the dire wolves. "Even from here, I can tell what happened. Those cats attacked the Yeti when he still had your wife in his hand. He put her down and fought the cats. She started to run away but then she ran back to the Yeti probably for protection. The Yeti killed the cats, picked up your wife, then he continued to head south. The wolves are scavenging off the remains of the cats." Rodgers sighed. "We are upwind from them, so they haven't noticed us yet. We saw what happened when we came to close to the teratorns. We will have to drive well out of sight of the wolves before we cut back toward the Yeti tracks."

Henry was staring at the wolves and thinking about how close they were to the Yeti and Gina when he remembered another fairy tale. He turned to Rodgers. "You have seen typical wolves in action. Are normal wolves able to run as fast as these snowmobiles can go?"

Rodgers thought about the question for a minute. "I would think that they could run pretty darn close to the speed of these things but not for too long."

Henry pressed Rodgers. "For how long could they keep up with the snowmobiles? Do you think that they could keep up for about a quarter of a mile?"

Rodgers shrugged. "I would say that they could." The hunter stared at Henry. "What are you getting at, Henry?"

Henry took a deep breath. "The Yeti protected Gina from the cats. I am betting that he will protect her from other threats as well." He pointed to the dire wolves. "Have you ever seen Disney's Beauty and the Beast? There is that scene where Belle is attacked by wolves and the Beast fights them off to save her. We are going to reenact that scene right now." Henry shrugged. "Those are dire wolves. Like the teratorns, they hunted our ancestors. We don't know how far away from them we will have to drive to bypass them and we don't know what other things we may run into out there. If we run into more teratorns without a cave to run into, we know that we are dead. We know that the Yeti will protect Gina and we know that a typical wolf is able to more or less keep up with a snowmobile." Henry took another deep breath. "We are a little over a quarter mile away from Gina. We are going to ride past those wolves and get them to chase us to Gina and the Yeti. The Yeti put Gina down before to fight off the cats, hopefully he will do the same thing when faced with a pack of wolves."

Henry motioned for Jun-Tuk to climb off his snowmobile and to join Rodgers on his vehicle. Henry nodded. "When the Yeti puts Gina down and is engaged with the dire wolves, I will grab Gina and then we will make a wide arch away from the battle and head back to the valley pass."

Rodgers shook his head. "That's your plan? You are putting a lot of pure hope into that plan Henry. What if Gina dropped that transmitter and she and the Yeti are miles, if not days, ahead of us? What if those wolves can run faster than the snowmobiles? What if the Yeti does not put Gina down? What if the wolves ignore the Yeti and go right for the easier prey in Gina?"

Rodgers voice rose to just under a yell. "What about your Eskimo friend here? He wants to bring back proof that the Yeti is just an animal. The only way that we can bring that proof back is if we kill the Yeti ourselves. All of these points seem moot however, when you consider that the basis for your plan is a child's cartoon!"

Henry glared at Rodgers. "The plan is based on the information that we have available to us. Jun-Tuk's proof will come when we blow the sides of the valley pass and the Yeti stops attacking his village." Henry took a step a closer to the hunter. "The only thing that my plan excludes is giving you a shot at the Yeti. After seeing how the wooly rhino and the teratorns handled our rifles, I am not overly inclined to think that we can take down that monster."

Rodgers sneered. "It's a suicide plan. I won't be a part of it."

Henry shrugged. "Then you better start hauling ass back to the pass because I am going to anger some dire wolves."

Henry revved his snowmobile then he went speeding toward the dire wolves. Rodgers cursed and followed him just like Henry knew that he would. The hunter was determined to get a shot at the Yeti no matter what. There was no way that Rodgers would risk letting a pack of giant wolves steal his prize from him.

As Henry was closing in on the six dire wolves, the beasts looked up from their feast and stared at the approaching oddity of the snowmobiles. When Henry was able to get a closer look at the wolves, they terrified him even more than they had through his binoculars. Henry sped past one of the wolves as it chewed on a piece of the dead cat. He could see that each of its teeth was as long as a steak knife and three times as thick. He also got a good look at jaws that looked more than powerful enough to tear his head off with a single bite. Henry sped past the wolves and he screamed and hollered at them in order to gain their attention. Rodgers was a second behind Henry, and while the sulking hunter remained silent, Henry could hear Jun-Tuk screaming as well. Henry had not taken the time to translate the plan to Jun-Tuk but he was glad that the old man trusted him enough to follow his lead.

The snowmobiles had no sooner passed the dire wolves than the fearsome animals started growling and cashing after them. Henry pushed his snowmobile to its full speed. He knew that his plan was risky and that there was a chance that it could get them all killed. He also thought that despite all of the mistakes that he made during this expedition, that this was the most sound information based decision that he had made. When Henry heard the barking of the dire wolves getting closer to him, he prayed that if nothing else that his plan would let him see Gina one last time before he died.

CHAPTER 15

Gina couldn't sleep. Yukon, Wen-Ku, even Thu-Ca were all sound asleep but Gina was too preoccupied with waiting for a chance to make a break for it. She looked toward the opening of the cave. From the sunlight that poured into the cave, Gina guessed that it had to be around twelve noon. Wen-Ku had said that the crawling demons did not like the light. If Wen-Ku's assertion was true, then it would make sense that it would be safer for them to sleep near the mouth of the cave when the sun was out. Gina hoped that the smell of the meat she had placed in the cave walls would entice at least one of the crawling demons to venture slightly closer to the light for an easy meal.

Gina continued to stay close to Yukon and to stare at the deeper recess of the vast cave. She was stretching her senses to the limit in an attempt to hear or see something making its way toward them. Gina also hoped that whatever found the hidden meat would be large enough to draw Yukon's attention long enough for her to grab the baby and run out into the valley.

She had thought that she heard something scratching the walls but the sound quickly ended and Gina convinced herself that the sound was only her imagination. A few seconds later, she heard the sound again and this time she was sure that it was not her imagination. She focused her vision as much as she could. Gina's heart raced when she saw a large round shadow in the flickering lights of the dying torches. The sound that she heard changed from a scratch to more of a tearing sound. Gina started to say a prayer that Yukon would hear the sound and wake up to investigate it. She groaned to herself at the irony of praying that a perceived god would wake up and defend her from a so-called demon. The thought had no sooner crossed Gina's mind when Yukon's eyes snapped open. The Yeti quickly scooped up both Gina and Wen-Ku in his powerful claw and pushed them behind him. Yukon growled at the shadow, and when he did so, the shadow turned and faced the direction of the cave opening.

Gina could hear something walking toward them as the shadow of the unknown beast continued to bounce along the cave wall. Gina heard a hissing sound and then she screamed when she saw a gargantuan rat come crawling out of the tunnel. Gina quickly sized up the rat. She estimated that it was a little more than two thirds the size of Yukon. She figured that the rat was roughly fifteen feet tall.

Yukon roared at the giant rat and then the Yeti took a step backwards. It was the first time that Gina had seen the Yeti back away from any threat. As an anthropologist, Gina had run into many a rat in tight places and she was well aware that even a normal a rat could be a nasty customer in a tight space. The cave was big and Yukon had some room to maneuver but Gina was sure that the giant rat was better adapted to fighting in the cave then the Yeti was. From Wen-Ku's description, Gina had guessed that one of the species that she called the crawling demons could be some form of rat. She had just prayed that either her assumption was wrong or that one of the other crawling demons would be the first to show up.

Yukon roared at the rat, and as he did so, the Yeti took another step backward but this time he also took a step closer to the cave wall. Gina gasped when she saw where Yukon had positioned himself. The Yeti had not been backing away from the giant rat out of fear. The Yeti had been making sure that his body was in front of the crevice where Thu-Ca was hidden. Gina had seen Yukon charge every other beast that he had faced. She knew that if a creature was to come out of the cave system that it would have to come at them from a distance. When the cave bear had entered the cave, Yukon had charged the monster. Gina had not considered the fact that when the cave bear had attacked that Thu-Ca was deep in the cave. It seemed that when the infant was close to the danger, the Yeti was determined to make sure that he was safe. Gina's escape plan included grabbing Thu-Ca when Yukon charged a looming threat but the Yeti had surprised her by taking a completely different approach when the infant was nearby.

Gina was lost in thought when Wen-Ku grabbed her arm and pulled her into the sunlight at the mouth of the cave. The native woman whispered to Gina. "The sunlight will keep us safe and the

Yeti god shall protect Thu-Ca. We must stay clear of the battle so that the Yeti god will not have to concern himself with inadvertently hurting us as he fights off the crawling demon." Wen-Ku then pulled Gina behind a large stalagmite that was bathed in sunlight.

The giant rat hissed again and Yukon growled in reply and stood his ground. The rat moved forward in a flash of fur and teeth. Gina's eyes had barely registered that the creature had moved before it had reached Yukon. The rat stood up on its hind legs and then sank its two-foot-long incisors into Yukon's shoulder. The Yeti roared in pain as the rat shook his head from side to side in an attempt to tear Yukon's arm off. Blood spurted out of the Yeti's shoulder like a geyser spraying both the cave wall and the rat in the life-sustaining fluid. Yukon shook his head in anger then he wrapped his arms around the rat. With a powerful heave, Yukon tossed the foul beast into the cave wall. The giant rat bounced off the wall and onto the cave floor. The rodent hissed at the Yeti and took a few steps backwards.

It was evident to Gina that the rat had the advantage in speed and agility, but Yukon was by far the stronger of the two monsters. Yukon roared at the rat in another attempt to scare the creature off. The rat hissed then it charged the Yeti again. Yukon was prepared for the rat's attack, and when the rat reared up on its hind legs, Yukon's arms shot out and the monster grabbed the rodent by the neck and right claw. For a second time, Yukon threw the rat into the cave wall and once more the rat ricocheted off the wall and onto the cave floor. The gargantuan rodent repeated the process of hissing and preparing to charge the Yeti.

Gina could see how this battle was going to play itself out. The rat would continue to charge Yukon and he would continue to catch the rat and slam it into the wall until the rat's neck broke or its skull cracked open. Gina looked behind her at the wide open cave entrance into the valley. She considered the fact that Yukon was occupied and that she could run into the valley without fear of the Yeti chasing her. Every sensible thought in her mind told her to run now, to leave Yukon behind, and to try and find Henry. Gina was thinking about running when she heard Thu-Ca crying from within the crevice in the cave wall. Gina's heart sank when she heard the baby cry. She knew that she would not be able to live with herself if she left the baby with Yukon. She watched as the rat charged Yukon again and for the third time the Yeti grabbed the rat and threw it into the cave wall. This time the rat stumbled after it bounced off the wall. Gina was sure that the horrid creature could not take more than one or two more slams into the wall before it finally died. Gina's opportunity to escape was quickly slipping away from her. She realized that she needed to change the dynamic of the battle if she had any hope of grabbing Thu-Ca and making a run into the valley.

Gina remembered Yukon's battle with the saber-toothed cats and how the Yeti had positioned himself between her and the cats to protect her. She hoped that he would do so again, and if not, she decided that she would run out into the sunlight as fast as she could and pray that it was enough to scare off the rat. Gina jumped out from behind the stalagmite, waved her arms, and screamed, "Over here you overgrown rodent! There is a much easier meal right here!" Gina's pulse was racing as she sprinted to the far side of the cave. The giant rat followed her with its eyes as she ran. When Gina reached the far wall, she turned to see a look of fear and concern on Yukon's face. Once more, the Yeti had surprised her by appearing to exhibit much more human-like emotions than she would have thought the monster capable of possessing.

Gina's attention was brought back to the rat when she saw a streak of brown moving toward her. The rat didn't make a sound. The monster simply ran toward Gina. Gina saw the rat coming for her and behind it she saw Yukon racing after the beast. Gina ran behind and around the nearest stalagmite. Her sharp turn caused the rat to slide into the cave wall. Gina ran past Yukon and toward the crevice that held the screaming Thu-Ca. Yukon turned to look at Gina as she ran past him and it provided that giant rat with the opportunity to pounce on the Yeti and drive its incisors into the Yeti's hip. Yukon howled in pain, and when Gina saw the rat latched onto him, she pulled Thu-Ca out of the crevice. Gina then turned and ran to the front of the cave.

Yukon was pounding on the rat's head and neck when Gina stopped at the front of the cave and grabbed a blanket that she wrapped the baby in. She was about to run out into the valley when Wen-Ku stepped in front of her. The native women yelled, "What are you doing? Thu-Ca must stay here in the cave of the Yeti and so must you and your child. Our children are heirs to the Yeti's power!"

Gina didn't waste time arguing with the misguided woman. Instead, she delivered a roundhouse kick to Wen-Ku's temple. Wen-Ku fell to the ground like a ragdoll and Gina quickly stepped over her and ran out into the valley.

Wen-Ku was lying on the floor and looking at Yukon when the Yeti saw Gina run out of the cave with Thu-Ca. Wen-Ku was forced to cover her ears as the monster unleashed a roar that shook the entire cave. The Yeti then grabbed the rat, lifted it over his head, and then he slammed the giant rodent directly on top of a large stalagmite. Blood poured out of the rat and pooled around Yukon's feet. The rodent squealed and convulsed as it tried in vain to free itself from the pointed rock that penetrated its body. Yukon looked and that creature in disgust. He then lifted his massive foot off the ground and brought it crashing down on the giant rat's head. The Yeti's stomp crushed the rat's skull flat sending a mixture of blood and grey matter splattering around the cave.

Yukon lifted his foot out of the gore that had been his opponent's head. The Yeti roared once more and then he ran out of the cave. Wen-Ku followed Yukon into the valley. She had expected to see Gina sprinting away from the cave with the Yeti god in close pursuit. Instead, she found both Gina and Yukon standing in the snow and looking to the north. Their eyes were fixed on two snowmobiles that were less than thirty feet away from them and only a few feet behind the snowmobiles was a hungry pack of dire wolves.

CHAPTER 16

Gina felt as if she was moving in a dream. Everything around her appeared as if it was happening in slow motion. It was the same feeling that she had when her body entered what is known as a *runner's high* amongst joggers. It's a state of euphoria that is attained by the combined release of adrenaline and endorphins. The sight of Henry, her husband and the father of her child, speeding toward her filled Gina's mind with a sense of joy and hope that was beyond the capabilities of words to describe. The sense of joy was at the same time countered by a rush of fear at the sight of the pack of dire wolves quickly closing on Henry. Gina could see Henry yelling and reaching his arm out for her as he slowly came closer to her. She reached out in return for him and she thought that in a matter of seconds, she would be speeding away from this nightmare.

Gina's mind barely registered that ground was shaking around her as Yukon stepped over her and growled at the oncoming snowmobiles and wolf pack. Henry, Rodgers and Jun-Tuk had nearly reached Gina when Yukon stepped over her, and with two quick swipes of his claws, he knocked both of the snowmobiles to the ground. When the snowmobiles toppled, they sent their passengers tumbling through the snow. The Yeti was facing Henry and he was in mid-roar when two dire wolves jumped onto the Yeti's chest and two more latched onto his legs with their fangs.

Henry and Rodgers each grabbed a pack off their snowmobiles as well as their weapons. Rodgers yelled, "Into the cave!" He and Jun-Tuk ran into the cave while Henry grabbed Gina. He looked at the baby in her arms with surprise, then he pulled her into the cave. Rodgers and Jun-Tuk ducked behind a stalagmite where they watched the primal battle taking place outside of the cave. The dire wolves were tearing into Yukon. The Yeti would grab a wolf and toss it, only to have another wolf take its place.

Henry saw a native woman starting to sit up at the side of the cave. He turned to Rodgers. "I think that Gina is in shock. Watch her and the baby. I have got to save that woman."

Henry stood up when Gina reached out and grabbed him. "No, leave her alone. She is totally devoted to Yukon." Henry stared at his wife with a confused look on his face. Gina sighed. "The Yeti. I named him Yukon. That woman believes that she is his bride. This is her son who she also believes is the son of Yukon. Yukon was an alpha male Yeti who was dethroned. Since then, he has been trying to build a new family for himself by going to Jun-Tuk's tribe to take pregnant women. He also takes women who are not pregnant to help take care of the mothers after they give birth. When the mothers are recovered, Yukon returns the helpers. The mothers and the infants stay but they have all been killed by the monsters that live here in the valley. That woman feels though that she and the baby must stay here. That is why I was trying to save the baby."

Henry nodded and pointed to the furious battle raging outside of the cave. He watched in awe as despite the fact that Yukon had two dire wolves attached to his chest, that he was still able to lift a third wolf over his head and throw it at two of its fellow pack members. The wolf and the two beasts that it hit went tumbling through the snow. Yukon then brushed two of the other wolves off his broad chest as if they were flies. Another wolf lunged at Yukon's leg and the Yeti bent down and swatted the massive canine aside. He stood up just as the three wolves he had knocked down sprang back at his legs and chest.

Henry pointed to the mouth of the cave with his rifle. "We will just wait for the battle to finish. We have enough ammunition to take out the dire wolves if any of them survive. It looks like that Yeti is already hurt I can see numerous wounds on him. We might even be able to take him down if he wins the battle and he is injured badly enough."

Gina shook her head as Yukon lifted up another dire wolf and tossed it away from him. "All of those cuts are little more than flesh wounds to that monster. I have seen all types of beasts bite and scratch him over the past two days. Yukon's muscles and bones must be incredibly dense. I have seen monsters with teeth over a foot long bite into him and still not hit anything vital." Gina sighed. "Those wolves don't have a prayer. All that they are going to do is cut and anger him. It may take him some time, but he will crush them like he has everything else that he has come across and he will be none the worse for it." She gestured to Henry's rifle. "I doubt that your weapons will have much more effect on him than any of the claws or teeth of the creatures that he has slain so far. He will kill the wolves and then he will come in here and kill you three as well." Gina heard a wolf yelp and she quickly looked back at the battle taking place outside of the cave. She could see three of the dire wolves tearing into Yukon's legs as he grabbed a fourth wolf by its neck and rear hips. Yukon then lifted it over his head. The Yeti roared then he ripped the helpless wolf in half. Yukon was showered in blood and entrails as he used the two halves of the bisected wolf to beat back the other dire wolves from his legs. Gina pointed to the back of the cave. "Our only hope of getting out of here is through the tunnels. They run throughout the entire mountain range. We can use them to make our way back to the valley pass."

Henry shook his head. "There are giant millipedes in the caves. They killed several of our team members when we stopped in one of the caves on the way here. Once we escaped them, I sent Dana and Gordon back with the survivors. I told them to start evacuating base camp when they got back."

Gina pointed outside as Yukon lifted up a dire wolf in each of his hands and tossed them. He then lifted his foot and stomped on a third wolf, crushing it with his tremendous weight. Gina yelled, "Trust me! I have seen Yukon in action and I know what monsters are in the tunnels. Yukon is destroying those wolves and then he will come in here for us. He will follow us through the tunnels and yes, we may have to fight our way through some of the monsters in there, but we have weapons." She grabbed two of the flares from Henry's bag. "We also have flares and torches. The monsters in the tunnels are sensitive to light. If we can slip past them, Yukon will have to fight through those same monsters without the benefit of light. Yukon can move like a freight train at full speed. Let's grab some torches and get going before he gets back in here! The more of a head start that we have on him, the better our chances of survival are."

Henry looked at his wife and he could see the conviction in her eyes. He knew how intelligent she was. He had also been with her long enough to know when she was sure that her plan was the best option to follow. He loved her and more than that, he trusted her. He ran to the wall and grabbed several torches. "Alright, but we only to need to take the tunnels about half way back to the valley pass. We didn't see any other caves other than the one that we stayed in and the cave that we found you in. Outside of the first cave, there are several snowmobiles that we can use to make it back to the valley pass. We just have to keep heading north through the tunnels until we find the next cave opening. It should be the cave that the snowmobiles are outside of. As long as we can avoid the teratorns, the snowmobiles are the safest and quickest way for us to get out of here." Gina nodded and stood. Once more, Jun-Tuk followed the Murella's lead but Rodgers started moving closer to the mouth of the cave.

Gina yelled at him, "Rodgers, come on!"

He smiled. "You cowards run into the tunnels. I came here for that Yeti and I am going to kill him. When he is dead, I'll yell for you to come out of the tunnels and then we can all go home with my trophy."

Gina went argue with him when Henry grabbed her. "He is insane. We would be wasting our time arguing with him." Gina nodded then she switched the baby to her left hand and grabbed a torch with her right. Jun-Tuk and Henry each slung their weapons over their shoulders then they each grabbed a flickering torch in both of their hands. They nodded and then they started walking into the tunnel system with Gina behind them.

Rodgers crawled closer to the mouth of the cave as the struggle between Yukon and the remaining dire wolves raged on. Rodgers saw the native woman standing next to edge of the cave staring at him but she was unarmed and presented no threat to him. Rodgers crouched down next to a stalagmite and watched as the remaining four dire wolves continued to attack Yukon. The four wolves were gathered around the Yeti's legs. Two wolves were tearing into each of the Yukon's legs and the Yeti kept swatting them off. With a swipe from his claw, Yukon knocked away both wolves that were attacking his right leg. He then made a fist and brought it down onto the back of one of the wolves that was attacking his left leg. Rodgers heard a loud crack that he was sure was the dire wolf's spine snapping in half. The dead wolf fell to the ground. Yukon then reached down and grabbed the second wolf that was still attacking his left leg. The monster lifted the wolf over his head then he turned and faced the cave. Yukon threw the wolf into the rock wall that made up the edge of the cave entrance. The Yeti threw the wolf with such force that when the canine struck the wall, most of the bones on the left side of its body shattered. The dead wolf slid down the outside of the cave wall as the remaining two wolves continued to foolishly attack Yukon.

The remaining two wolves sprang at Yukon again. The first wolf jumped onto Yukon's chest while the second one continued to attack the Yeti's leg. The first wolf was biting and clawing at Yukon's chest until the Yeti wrapped his powerful arms around the animal. Rodgers watched as Yukon squeezed the dire wolf so hard that its midsection collapsed, its eyes budged out of its head, and several other organs shot out of its mouth. Yukon dropped the dead dire wolf then he reached down and picked up the one remaining wolf by the scruff of its neck. Yukon lifted the canine up to his eye level and he roared at it. He then latched his jaws onto the dire wolf's throat and tore it out.

Rodgers was in awe at the power and ferocity of Yukon as the Yeti threw his arms out in front of himself and roared proclaiming his victory to the world. The Yeti was drenched in blood and entrails as he turned back toward the cave. Rodgers readied his rifle for the kill of his life when to his left he saw the native women laughing at him. He sneered. "We will see who is laughing in a few seconds after I kill your god."

Yukon entered the cave and Rodgers slowed down his breathing and slowly positioned his rifle under his arm and along his chin. He took aim directly at the Yeti's right eye and was slowly squeezing the trigger when the native screamed causing Yukon to turn his head to the side. The slight movement caused Rodgers's bullet to strike Yukon in the side of his head rather than in his eye. The Yeti roared and grabbed his head before turning in Rodgers' direction. Rodgers didn't take to time to aim. The hunter just started firing wildly at Yukon. Rodgers could see the bullets burying themselves in the Yeti's skin but he could also see that they were causing no real damage. Yukon charged toward Rodgers and the hunter sprinted across the cave and into a series of stalagmite that dotted the left hand side of the cave.

Rodgers ducked behind a stalagmite. He then peered out from behind it and fired another shot into the center of the Yeti's chest. As before, the bullet penetrated the monster's skin but it failed to make it through the beast's thick muscles and into its heart. Rodgers screamed as he continued to fire at the Yeti. Yukon roared in pain and anger as each bullet tore its way through his skin. He ran over to the rows of stalagmite and he started smashing them as he forced Rodgers closer to the cave wall. Rodgers was walking backwards as a rain of rock poured down on him from the stalagmite that Yukon was smashing his way through. Rodgers continued to step backward until he felt his body connect with the cave wall. He instinctively lifted his rifle and fired his last two bullets into Yukon's right shoulder. Rodgers squeezed his rifle again to hear the harrowing click of an empty rifle.

The hunter looked up into the enraged red eyes of the Yeti who was standing above him. The monster stared down at Rodgers and growled at him. Rodgers had been a hunter for his entire life. During his career, he had been stalked by lions, bears, and countless other predators. As recently as the previous day, he had been attacked by teratorns, a wooly rhino, and giant millipedes. In all of those instances, he still felt some sense of control. He knew that he was in danger, but he was confident that by keeping his wits he could escape the situation alive. This time, however, he knew that he was going to die. Rodgers now knew how all of the animals felt that turned to see him pointing his rifle at them right before he pulled the trigger. With his death at hand, Rodgers' pride swelled up inside of him. He pulled his hunting knife out of his pocket and yelled at the giant towering over him, "Come on then! Finish it!"

Rodgers ran forward wielding his knife in front of him. Yukon roared at the tiny creature that dared to attack him in his own home. The Yeti lifted his fist over his head and brought it crashing down on top of Rodgers. When the monster lifted his hand up, all that remained of Rodgers was a smear of blood, bones, and organs on the cave floor.

Yukon roared then he looked to the back of the cave in the direction that Gina, Henry, and Jun-Tuk had taken Thu-Ca. Wen-Ku pulled two torches off the wall and then she walked over next to Yukon. "Yes, they have taken our children. I will carry the light for you to help keep the crawling demons at bay. We shall track down those who dared to take our children from us. You shall kill the two men, and then we shall bring back Thu-Ca as well as your other bride and the child that she carries within her."

Wen-Ku started walking deep into the cave, and when Yukon realized what she was doing, the huge Yeti picked up the Quinic woman in his hand. With his bride within his hand and torch in her grasp, the Yeti started sprinting through the massive tunnel system after Gina and her unborn child.

CHAPTER 17

Gordon had Dana wrapped around his waist as he continued to lead the remaining team members back to the valley pass. The sun was at its highest point and Gordon figured that it was roughly noon. He was pushing the remaining snowmobiles at full speed and he was sure that the vehicles would run out of gasoline shortly after they exited the valley pass. He figured that the team could hike back to campsite after they had made it out of the valley. The important thing right now was to get everyone out of the valley alive. Gordon was staying close to the base of the mountains when he saw movement along the mountain slope to his left. It was difficult to discern what he was seeing at first. When he took a closer look, the hunter quickly made out two camouflaged animals making their way down the side of mountain in the direction the snowmobiles were headed. Gordon yelled to Dana, "Reach up and grab the steering. Then slowly start having us move away from the base of the mountain. Move the snowmobile slow and steady, nothing sudden." Gordon lifted his rifle up to his face. "There are some kind of predators stalking us along the mountainside. They are going to attack us when they cross our path in about thirty seconds." He loaded his rifle. "I am going to try to shoot them before they attack us." He took one more look at Dana. "No one else dies. Everyone still left breathing is going to get out of this valley alive."

Dana took the controls and she started moving the snowmobile away from the base of the mountain in order to buy them a few extra seconds. Gordon looked through the scope of his rifle to see two snow white cats with incredibly long canine teeth sprinting down the side of the mountain. Like everything else in the valley the cats were huge. The saber-toothed cats dwarfed even the largest lions that Gordon had hunted in Africa. Gordon took aim at the first saber-toothed cat and he squeezed his trigger. Gordon watched as the cat's body shuddered and blood spurted from its shoulder.

Gordon took aim once again at the injured saber-toothed cat as its hunting partner continued to make its way down the mountainside at a full sprint. Gordon quickly fired four more shots at the injured predator. The first two shots missed but the other two shots hit the beast in the neck and head instantly killing the cat. The second cat was only a few steps away from them and Gordon had its head in his sights. He went to pull the trigger but the snowmobile ran over a snow-covered rock which caused Gordon's shot to go high over the cat's head. The massive cat was only a few seconds away from reaching the snowmobile and sinking its long teeth into Dana's back.

Gordon didn't think. He just reacted. The hunter jumped at the same time that the saber-toothed cat pounced at the snowmobile. Gordon's body slammed into the cat in mid-air. The impact of Gordon's body managed to slow down the cat's momentum enough that the monster missed Dana's snowmobile. Gordon landed face first in the snow. He heard and felt the snowmobiles of his team members whipping by him. He then felt something warm and sticky sliding down the back of his neck. He rolled over to see the saber tooth cat standing above him and drooling.

The second that Dana saw Gordon jump off the snowmobile, she turned around. The young doctor saw the other team members coming toward her and she yelled, "Don't stop! Keep heading north for the valley pass." Dana watched as Gordon tried to lift his rifle to shoot the cat but the monster growled and swatted the rifle out of Gordon's hands. Dana reached into her pocket and pulled out one of the flares that she had grabbed earlier. She lit the flare and drove directly at Gordon and the saber-toothed cat.

Gordon looked up at the cat as it growled above him. In an act of desperation, Gordon reached down to his leg and pulled his hunting knife out of its sheath. The cat growled and then brought its teeth down toward Gordon. The hunter threw his forearm in front of himself. He was able to get his left forearm under the cat's long saber-like canines but the animal still managed to close its teeth around Gordon's forearm. Gordon screamed in pain as the cat's jaws closed around his arm simultaneously tearing through his skin and breaking his forearm in several places. The cat shook

Gordon's arm then it lifted its claw off the ground as it prepared to eviscerate the young hunter.

The cat was about to swipe its claw across Gordon's stomach when Dana drove up to the beast and threw the lit flare directly into its eyes. The beast growled and released its grip on Gordon's arm. The hunter didn't waste time waiting for the monster to recover. He brought his knife up and used it to slash the saber toothed cat's throat open. The ancient predator shook its head and backed up as its blood poured into its lungs, causing the monster to choke. Gordon crawled through the waterfall of blood that was pouring out of the cat's throat as he moved away from the predator. Dana pulled her snowmobile to a stop next Gordon. She helped the hunter to climb onto the back of the snowmobile and she shouted, "Hold on to me! We are only about twenty minutes from the valley pass!"

Gordon nodded and he wrapped his good arm around Dana's waist. She could tell how badly injured he was by the fact that the hunter's normally strong grip was as weak as a child's. Dana sent the snowmobile into high speed. First, she yelled to Gordon, "Try to keep your injured arm as elevated as possible. It will help to slow the bleeding!" She then did her best to continue steering the snowmobile while at the same time fishing the radio out of her pocket. When she finally found the radio, she turned it on and shouted, "Come in, base camp! This is Doctor Dana Summers. I am about fifteen minutes from exiting the valley. I need a Sno-Cat to meet us as close to the valley pass as possible with an emergency medical kit! Tony Gordon has been severely injured." Dana stopping talking for a minute. She had feared that the mountains around her might be blocking her radio signal. She shouted into the radio again, "I repeat, this is Doctor Dana Summers and I need a Sno-Cat with an emergency medical kit to meet us at the entrance to the valley pass. Do you copy?"

Dana was quite for a moment as she heard mainly static coming through the radio. She started to tear up in fear for Gordon's life when she heard a broken transmission come back through the radio. The signal was too weak for Dana to make out what the person on the other end of the transmission was saying. It could have been anything from *Message received, we will meet you at*

the pass to *We can't hear you. Your transmission is breaking up.*
She heard Gordon groan behind her and she could also feel his already light grip lessening around her waist. Dana gripped onto her lover as the exit to the valley pass finally came into view. She could see the remaining team members ahead of her making for the pass. Several minutes later, she saw the snowmobiles ahead of her exit the valley. She yelled to Gordon, "Tony, the rest of the team members made it out of the valley. We didn't lose anyone else."

She listened for some sort of reply but she didn't hear anything. She reached down and grabbed Gordon's wrist. She was relieved when she could still feel his pulse. Gordon was alive but he had passed out and he was still losing blood quickly. She was less than a hundred yards from the exit to the valley pass when the snowmobile started to sputter. The machine coughed a few times and then its engine stopped. Dana held onto Gordon and she steered the sliding snowmobile as far as she could before it finally came to a stop roughly fifty yards from the valley pass. Dana climbed off the snowmobile then she put Gordon's uninjured arm over her shoulder. She spoke to Gordon as gently as she could, "Come on, Tony, help me. You are too heavy for me to carry." Gordon's head lolled from side to side in an attempt to nod. He then started walking and bearing some of his weight. Dana had helped Gordon walk to within forty yards of the valley pass when the shadow of a gigantic bird fell over them.

In an instant, Dana assessed her situation; Gordon was too heavy for her to pick up and run with, she had no weapons, and she was still roughly thirty yards from exiting the valley. The shadow was growing larger, meaning that the teratorn was directly above them and descending quickly. When the teratorn's shadow had completely covered them Dana threw herself and Gordon to the left and to the ground. The teratorn's claws tore away a huge chunk of snow in the spot where the young lovers were only a moment before. The bird stood in the snow and then it turned to look at Dana and the unconscious Gordon. Dana closed her eyes and held onto Gordon as the teratorn lumbered toward them.

Dana was prepared to die when she heard shouting behind her. She looked to the valley pass to see the students who had just exited the valley running back through the pass. The team members had lit the remaining flares and they were holding them in their hands. The team members ran forward and hurled the burning flares at the teratorn. The bird squawked as the burning flares struck it. The teratorn took a step back and then it took to the air. Two of the male team members picked up Gordon and carried him to the valley pass while a young female helped Dana to her feet. Dana looked behind her and she saw the teratorn circle back around through the sky and then head straight for them. Dana yelled, "Run!" The team members all sprinted as fast as they could toward the valley pass while the teratorn quickly closed on them. Dana could see the teratorn's shadow over her as she entered the pass and then the shadow peeled off. The doctor felt a rush of wind across her face and she knew that she had reached the naturally occurring wind gusts that kept the teratorns from leaving the valley.

The girl who had helped Dana hugged her. "The snowmobiles all ran out of gas shortly after we got out of the valley. When we noticed that you and Mr. Gordon were not with us, we ran back to get you. There was no way that we were leaving the two of you in that valley."

Dana hugged her back. "Thank you." She turned to the two men holding Gordon. "Thank you all." She pointed at Gordon, "We have to get him back to camp before he bleeds to death." The two men nodded and then they started hiking back in the direction of camp. The crew had hiked for nearly ten minutes until they heard a noise ahead of them. Dana looked up to see one of the Sno-Cats coming toward them. They all cheered and Dana ran up to vehicle. She yelled at the men carrying Gordon, "Get him on board! I am going to perform emergency surgery on him on the way back to camp!"

The door to the Sno-Cat flew open and the driver said, "We got your message, Doctor Summers. We have an emergency med kit in the back of the cat."

The two men carried Gordon into the back of the Sno-Cat and placed him on the large floor used to carry supplies. Dana immediately tore Gordon's coat off. She then tied a tunicate around the upper part of his arm. Next, the doctor injected Gordon with a sedative to make sure that he stayed asleep. Then she quickly cleaned out his arm with an antiseptic. Once his arm was clean, she began resetting it and stapling his wounds shut. When she was finished, she sat back and took a deep breath.

One of the men who had helped carry Gordon into the Sno-Cat walked over to Dana. "Is he going to make it?"

She smiled. "I think so but I need to get him back to the ship for a blood transfusion." She ran up to the driver of the Sno-Cat. "We need to start getting everyone back to the ship and I want myself and this man on the first boat. We are all evacuating this area ASAP." She paused for a minute as she remembered what else Henry had said. "The only people that I want working on something other than the evacuation are the demolitions experts. I want them rigging the sides of the valley pass to blow. We need to create an avalanche to seal that pass off forever."

The driver shook his head. "I can radio to have the demolition experts in place but the evacuation is not going to happen, ma'am."

Dana shook her head. "What do you mean that the evacuation is not going to happen? Radio the crew on the ship and have them start sending the transport boats to shore."

The driver shrugged. "They couldn't send the boats even if they wanted to."

Dana screamed, "Why is that!"

They had reached the campsite and the driver pointed out the window. "See for yourself."

Dana looked out the window at the beach to see hundreds if not thousands of seals moving frantically around on the beach with the ship in the distance behind them. The animals covered the beach for as far as she could see leaving no place for the boats to land. She couldn't understand why the seals were all on shore and so disturbed. Then she noticed the dozens of long black fins moving along the surface of the water. She whispered, "The orcas."

The driver pulled the Sno-Cat to a stop as they arrived in camp. "The orcas have driven the seals onto the only stretch of beach that is not too rocky for the transport boats to land. The orcas will wait until the seals are hungry enough to try and venture out into the surf for fish. Then the orcas will rush the beach and grab as many of the seals as they can. This standoff could take hours, and in the meantime, there are too many damn seals for the boats to land. Even if they tried to force their way through the seals, the damn things would tear up the boats' propellers and then we would really be stuck here." The driver shrugged. "We aren't going anywhere for a while."

CHAPTER 18

The torch that Gina held was starting to flicker out and Thu-Ca was crying. Gina shook her head knowing that those two factors were only going to increase the likelihood that they were going to run into some monster in the dark tunnels. Henry ran in front of Gina and Jun-Tuk was behind her as the two men did their best to protect both her and the baby. Still, all three people knew that their prospects of survival were almost nonexistent. The tunnel that they were running through was still massive. It was easily wide enough and had a high enough ceiling for Yukon or any other of the monsters to run through it at full speed.

When they first entered the tunnels, Gina had asked the two men how much ammunition they each had left. Henry had about six bullets left and Jun-Tuk was not in a much better position. The old man had only eight arrows left for his crossbow. Gina figured that they had enough ammunition to fight off one of the giant rats that she had seen Yukon battle or a couple of the giant millipedes that Henry had briefly described to her. She had no idea if they had enough ammunition to deal with the third form of *crawling demon* that Wen-Ku had described. Gina had no doubt that if Yukon found them that they did not have anywhere near the firepower to kill the Yeti.

Their journey was made even more difficult by the fact that they were running through the heated tunnels in their arctic clothing. They were all sweating profusely and Gina worried that dehydration could set in on them at any moment. In addition to the crying baby, the heat, their dying lights, and limited ammunition they could only hope that they were following the tunnels in a northern direction. Gina was sure that their initial turn to the right was taking them back in the direction of the valley pass but the tunnel system had already taken a few subtle turns. She was still fairly confident that they were moving in the right direction. She also told herself that taking a chance in the tunnels was a better choice than facing certain death, which is what would have happened if they had tried to run past Yukon and the dire wolves.

They had been moving at a fast walk for over forty minutes when they heard a blood-curdling roar echo throughout the tunnels. The group stopped moving and simultaneously the torch that Gina was holding burned out. The tunnel became darker as Henry and Jun-Tuk's torches also continued to flicker. The roar echoed through the tunnel again and Gina looked at Henry. "That's Yukon. He must have defeated the dire wolves. From the sound of that roar, he is in the tunnel and coming after us. Between our scent and Thu-Ca's screaming, he will be able to find us without much difficulty."

Gina's heart began to race at the thought of Yukon killing Henry and Jun-Tuk and then carrying her back to his cave. Gina pulled Henry's arm. "Come on, we have to keep moving." The group ran through the tunnel and as they did so, one by one their torches started to burn out. Jun-Tuk had suggested that they keep the torches when they burned out because holding a club constructed of bone was better than having no weapon at all. Henry was holding the last torch as it slowly burned out. When the flame finally extinguished itself, Henry reached into his bag and pulled out one of the flares that Dana had grabbed during the millipede attack. He snapped the flare open and lit it. The flare cast a fluorescent orange glow throughout the large tunnel.

Gina looked at Henry. "How many more of those things do we have?"

Henry took a quick look in his supply bag, "Looks like we have two more after this. They each burn for about fifteen minutes. It took us about forty-five minutes to get from the area where the other snowmobiles are to here. We have been moving for a little over a half an hour on foot. If we don't take too many turns and we pick up the pace, we might just have enough flares to get us through this underground hell and back out into the light."

There was another roar behind them that sounded much closer than the last set of roars they had heard. Gina turned and broke into a full sprint away from the roar. Henry and Jun-Tuk found themselves behind Gina and they took off after her as quickly as they could. Henry could feel his legs burning as he did his best to stay close enough to his wife to give her enough light to avoid running face first into a wall.

Gina was running as fast as she could with the bright red glow of the burning flare illuminating the tunnel a few feet in front of her. She saw a flash of white in front of her and she skidded to a stop. Henry and Jun-Tuk also came to a stop behind her and Henry lifted his flare in front of him to see a huge interwoven lattice of some form of thick white rope. Gina looked around the tunnel to see that the white rope covered the entire tunnel. At a quick glance, she estimated that the tunnel was at least thirty feet wide and fifty feet high. Henry moved his light around and then Gina saw the dead form of a giant rat stuck in the top of the interwoven rope. The rat's body was nothing more than a dried out husk. The rat's corpse looked as if all of its bodily fluids had been drained out of it. Gina looked at the face of the dead giant rat and she immediately winced from the look of complete terror on the creature's face.

Gina gasped when it dawned on her exactly what they were looking at. She whispered to Henry. "Move the flare around so that it lights up the tunnel ceiling. Keep a close eye on the dark corners of this stuff." Henry slowly waved his flare above his head and all three people gasped when the light reflected off two sets of multi-faceted eyes. A massive hair-covered body with long legs jointed in the shape an arch came into view. A huge tarantula-like spider was watching the three humans from the upper most corner of its web. Henry shifted his flare to get a better look at the monster. When the light hit it the colossal arachnid that was curled up in a corner of the ceiling condensed its body even more at the sight of the bright light of the flare. Gina whispered, "The crawling demon that has legs like poles and lives in a net. A giant spider." A loud roar echoed behind the group and Gina could tell that Yukon was quickly closing on them. She took a look around the web and up at the spider. "That thing has to be, what, thirty to thirty five feet long?"

Henry stammered. "Yes. As soon as that thing makes a move, we are dead."

Gina shook her head and spoke quickly. "No, don't you see? That thing is exactly what we need!" She pointed up at the giant spider. "Look at that spider. It's terrified of the light from the flare. Also, most spiders will only attack things that disturb their webs."

She pointed to the foot thick web that connected to the tunnel wall in front of them. "Use the flare to burn through these three strands of web here. We will be able to slip through and keep going. We will leave Yukon to run face first into the web and then to deal with the spider while we continue to push ahead." There was another roar and all three people knew that Yukon would be upon them any second. Henry took his flare and he started burning through the web in front of them. The giant spider took a few steps out onto its web but it stopped when it saw the bright light of the flare. Jun-Tuk pointed his crossbow at the spider and Gina instructed him in his own language, "If it takes another step, shoot it in the eye." Jun-Tuk nodded and kept his weapon aimed at the spider.

Henry had burned through two of the pieces of web and he was working on the third strand when Yukon stormed around the corner. The Yeti roared and Wen-Ku screamed, "Stop! You are the bride of the Yeti god! You and the children must return to the cave with us!"

The flare finally burnt through the last strand of web and Henry screamed, "We are through. Let's move!" Henry moved through the opening first followed by Gina and Jun-Tuk. The three people sprinted farther down the tunnel and Yukon ran after them only to be stopped when he became caught in the giant web. The Yeti dropped Wen-Ku and when she hit the cave floor, her torch rolled away from her, leaving only a few strands of light illuminating the tunnel. Yukon roared then he started to pull the web off himself. The web had slowed down Yukon but the Yeti's strength was more than enough to tear the trap to pieces. Yukon ripped a large section of webbing off himself just as the giant spider crawled down what remained of the web and jumped on to Yukon. The Yeti was caught off balance and the weight of the spider forced him to the floor.

Yukon was laying on his back with the spider standing over him. The Yeti looked up to see the spider's fangs above him. Yukon's arm shot out and he grabbed the spider where its head connected to its body. The spider tried to force its head down but the strength of the Yeti was far greater than that of the spider. Yukon tossed the spider to his left. The arachnid stumbled to the side of the cave and Yukon used the opportunity to stand. Before the Yeti could renew his pursuit of Gina, the spider darted across the cave and attacked Yukon once more.

Yukon saw the spider charging him and he grabbed the spider's front legs immediately stopping its forward motion. The Yeti roared at the spider then he pulled it to him and stepped to the side so that the arachnid slammed into the wall. The spider quickly crawled up the side of the wall and over the top of Yukon. Yukon looked up just in time to see the spider dropping on top of him once more. The spider's weight slammed into Yukon and forced him to the ground again. Yukon was lying on his back with the spider over him again, preparing to inject him with its venom. Yukon moved in flash of white fur, and before the spider could strike him, the Yeti used his sharp claws to slice open the giant spider's underbelly. A thick yellow ichor poured out of the spider's mid-section as the monster backed away from the Yeti. The spider crawled to the cave wall and it was starting to scale it when Yukon threw his shoulder into the spider's back. The strength and weight of Yukon crushed the spider against the unforgiving cave wall and the arachnid burst like a child's water balloon. Yellow ichor sprayed across the tunnel and Yukon as the force from the Yeti's attack sent the bodily fluids of the giant spider flying in all directions.

Yukon shook himself once then he turned to see Wen-Ku holding her slowly dying torch. She was bloodied and bruised from her tumble onto the cave floor. Despite her injures, she smiled at her god/husband and said, "Well done. Now let us continue the pursuit of our children." Yukon reached down and picked up Wen-Ku then he started running farther through the massive tunnel system after what he perceived as his family.

CHAPTER 19

As Gina raced through the tunnel system, she could hear the battle between Yukon and the giant spider taking place behind them. Much like the battle with the dire wolves, Gina was already well-aware of the outcome of the conflict. Yukon would crush the spider just as he had every other creature that had dared to challenge him. In addition to the fact that Yukon would soon be pursuing them again, Thu-Ca was still screaming and Gina knew that the baby' cries would attract other predators. Gina knew that their chances of escaping the tunnels, let alone the valley, were slim. She took a brief look to her left at Henry running beside her. She considered telling Henry that she was pregnant. She thought if they were going to die, he should know that he was going to be a father or would that knowledge make the prospect of what they were facing even more difficult for him to bear?

She was about to tell him when she remembered how she felt when she learned that she was pregnant back in Yukon's cave. She recalled how learning that joyous new was tainted by the fact that she was trapped in a tunnel with a monster instead of in their home. She wanted Henry to have a better memory than that. She wanted to tell Henry in a special place like their home back in New Jersey or on a tropical beach when they were on vacation. She decided that Henry deserved to learn about their child in a better setting than in a cave filled with death and monsters. She also knew that the thought of making it through this nightmare to give Henry that news would help give her extra motivation to escape the valley. She looked over at Henry and she smiled because she knew how happy he would be when she was finally able to give him the news. Gina then looked ahead of her and she started running faster.

They had run for another five minutes until the flare that Henry was holding fizzled out. He reached into his pocket and pulled out another flare. He was about it light it when Gina said, "Wait. Look ahead of us." They could not see it with glow being given off by the last flare but just ahead of them was a small circle of light. Gina said, "That must be the other cave where the snowmobiles are at." They heard a roar and footsteps falling behind them. Henry lit the flare, and as soon as it illuminated the tunnel, they saw Yukon roughly five hundred yards behind them. The Yeti roared as he continued running toward them. Henry screamed, "Run!" The trio started to sprint through the tunnels toward the cave opening with Yukon quickly closing in on them. As they were running, Henry shouted, "What if the millipedes are still swarming in the cave? There is no way that we will be able to fight through all of them!"

Gina's mind was racing as she quickly reviewed everything that she had learned about the creatures in the tunnels so far. She handed the baby over to Jun-Tuk and took his crossbow from him. Gina noticed that as soon as she gave Thu-Ca to Jun-Tuk that the crying baby immediately calmed down. The old man bounced the baby slowly in his arms and Thu-Ca looked up at him and cooed. Gina somehow felt that Thu-Ca was meant to be with Jun-Tuk.

Gina pushed the thought aside and looked at Henry. "Quickly, give me the flare and the spare one in your bag." Henry quickly did as his wife instructed. Once Gina had the flares, he asked, "What are you going to with those things if the millipedes are still inside of the cave?"

Gina took a look a quick look behind her to see that Yukon was roughly two hundred yards behind them. She then snapped her head forward and guessed that they were about fifty yards from the cave opening. She thought to herself that, given the speed of the Yeti, it was going to be close if they were able to reach the back of the cave before the monster managed to catch up to them. She took a quick look over at Henry. "Let's hope that the millipedes are still in the cave because they are the only way that we are going to escape these tunnels."

They came to a sharp right in the tunnels that led into the cave. When Gina looked into the cave, she immediately saw dozens of giant millipedes crawling around the back and the center of the cave. She whispered a small thank you. She ran with a few feet of the giant millipede horde and threw the lit flare into their midst. At the sight of the blinding the light, the millipedes backed away from the burning flare to the sides of the cave wall. Gina dashed out into the opening followed by Henry and Jun-Tuk. Gina swung her head from side to side, and when she looked to her left, she saw one of the millipedes coming toward her. She fired her crossbow at the giant insect, hitting in the face and causing it to retreat a few feet. She looked in front of herself to see a wall millipedes forming. To her right, she saw Henry firing his few remaining bullets at millipedes that were hanging from the ceiling. Gina quickly lit her second flare and threw it at the millipedes that were massed in front of her. The wretched creatures once again scattered from the blinding light of the flare. Gina saw a small pathway open up in front of her to the exit of the cave. She heard a roar behind her and the entire cave shook as Yukon thundered into the back of the cave.

Gina didn't bother to look back. Instead, she just ran for the cave opening. Jun-Tuk ran closely behind her and Henry continued to fire his remaining bullets at any of the millipedes above or around them as they made their way to the cave exit. When they had ran out into the mid-afternoon sunlight, Gina quickly turned around to see Wen-Ku and Yukon standing near the first flare as it burned out. Wen-Ku yelled at Gina, "You must return to the Yeti god! You must raise his children..." The native women's sentence was cut off as the horde of millipedes enveloped both her and Yukon. Gina felt a wave of pity for the misguided woman who had just suffered a painful and horrible death.

Yukon howled, and from the sound of the howl, Gina knew that Yukon was not crying in pain from the millipedes that were attacking him. He was screaming out in anguish at the loss of Wen-Ku. Personally, Gina was glad to be away from the beast. Despite her personal feelings, the anthropologist in Gina was watching Yukon's reactions to experiences such as loss. Yukon's reactions to those experiences forced Gina to admit to herself that the Yeti's reactions to loss where more akin to a human than they were to an animal. She was still staring into the cave as a giant millipede climbed onto of the face of Yukon and bit into the top of his head. Even with the giant insect tearing into his head, Yukon continued to stare at Gina. Gina realized that as far as Yukon was concerned, his only remaining family consisted of herself, the baby inside of her, and Thu-Ca. With Wen-Ku dead, Yukon was watching as what remained of his family slipped away from him. Gina was mesmerized by the Yeti's gaze until Henry grabbed her arm. "Come on! We have to make for the snowmobiles and get out of here!"

Gina grabbed onto her husband's hand and they ran down the slope at the base of the mountain to the snowmobiles. Gina jumped onto one snowmobile and Jun-Tuk climbed on behind her with Thu-Ca in his arms. Henry climbed onto the other vehicle and they headed for the valley pass.

At the sight of Gina escaping with his family, Yukon went into a rage. The Yeti roared and he grabbed the millipede that was attacking his head. Yukon ripped the millipede off his head then he used it like a club to attack the other insects that were around him. Yukon threw the millipede carcass aside then he continued to tear into the millipedes that surrounded him. He picked a millipede that was in front of him and tossed into a group of other millipedes. The impact of the throw sent a half dozen of the insects tumbling to the cave wall. Several other millipedes wrapped themselves around Yukon's legs and midsection as two more of the giant insects fell onto top him from above. Yukon pulled the millipedes off his head then he tossed them into the cave wall with such force that the insects splatted against the rock when they hit it. The Yeti then grabbed the millipede on the right side of his body by its head. Yukon twisted the insect's head like a faucet handle until it tore free from the rest of its body. He then used his claw to slice open the back of the insect that was attached to his left side. Three more millipedes reared up in front of Yukon, and with one swipe of his claw, the Yeti cut them to pieces. Yukon began moving toward the cave entrance as the millipedes continued to attack him. The insects were large and their bites stung the mighty Yeti, but the millipedes were unable to do anything to Yukon expect to slow him down.

Like a juggernaut, Yukon hit, kicked, and clawed his way through the millipede horde as he made his way toward the cave entrance. The Yeti's snow-white fur took on a yellow tinge as it was drenched in the thick mucus-like fluid that ran through the insects' bodies. The cave was nearly a hundred yards long and even with the millipedes' relentless attack, it only took the powerful Yeti thirty seconds to make his way to the cave entrance. Just before he exited the cave, three of the giant millipedes fell on top of him from above. In a show of intelligence, Yukon ignored the insects and simply walked out into the subzero temperatures outside of the cave. When they were exposed to the cold, the millipedes let go of Yukon and fell writhing into the snow. Yukon could have crushed the insects beneath his huge feet, but instead the Yeti walked away from the horrible creatures. He was content to let them slowly freeze to death in the valley. The Yeti looked to the north to see Gina and the men who had helped her escape riding toward the valley pass on their snowmobiles. The Yeti snarled then he started running after what remained of his adopted family.

Yukon took long bounding steps. He was running faster than he had run after any previous prey. All that Yukon had that gave him comfort, that gave him a sense of belonging, and that made his solitary existence tolerable was quickly leaving him forever. The Yeti growled then he pushed his legs even harder to catch up to his bride and children.

CHAPTER 20

Gina and Henry were pushing their snowmobiles to the limit as they headed for the valley pass. Gina yelled over to Henry, "How much longer until we are out of here?"

Henry yelled back, "At this speed, we should be out of the valley in about twenty minutes!" He took a deep breath. "The only thing that we should have to worry about at this point is a teratorn attack! Jun-Tuk and I know from personal experience that they can fly faster than the snowmobiles can move!"

A roar echoed through the mountains behind them. Gina shook her head. "Teratorns are not the only thing that we have to worry about. That's Yukon. He will follow us all the way out of the valley and back to base camp." She gave a concerned look. "We can't lead that monster back to camp. If we do, more people will die when Yukon goes on a rampage through the camp as he looks for me and Thu-Ca."

Henry smiled. "There is no way that I am letting that monster get a hold of you or hurt anyone else." He gestured toward Gina's coat pocket. "Do you still have your radio?"

Gina quickly checked her pocket. "Yes, do you want me to tell them to make double-time evacuating the campsite back to the ship?"

Henry shook his head. "No. If we were to take off like that, Yukon might take his rampage to Jun-Tuk's village. When I sent back Dana and Gordon, in addition to starting the evacuation, I also told them to have the demolition experts rig the side of the mountain to cause an avalanche that will trap the Yeti in the valley forever. Get on your radio and tell them to hurry up. They have about a half an hour to blow the sides of the mountain before Yukon comes storming through the valley pass and heads to camp."

Gina grabbed her radio and switched it on. She knew that the demolition guys would be carrying radios because safety protocols demanded that they do so. She could never remember the two men's actual names. She had one time jokingly called them Axe and Smash after the old WWE tag team Demolition. The two guys got a good laugh out of it and had only referred to themselves as Axe and Smash whenever they were talking to Gina. She picked up her radio, "Axe, Smash, this is Professor Murella come in. Over."

There was static for a moment and then the gruff voice of Axe came back over the radio, "Professor Murella, you are alive! How are you? What happened? Is your husband with you?"

Gina spoke quickly, "Henry is with me. We are heading to the valley pass now. We should be there in roughly fifteen minutes. The Yeti is only a few minutes behind us. Do you have the charges set on the mountainside to seal off this valley?"

Axe spoke slowly, "We only have the charges set on the one side of the mountain. We thought that we were going to have more time."

Gina sighed. "Do you think that only blowing one side of the mountains will cause enough of an avalanche to completely block the valley pass?"

The radio was silent for a moment. "I can't say that it will completely block it, but it will sure make a mess of things."

Gina nodded to herself. "Okay, we will just have to go with that. We will be out of the valley in just over ten minutes. Can you get the minimum safe distance to blow the charges in that time?"

Axe was taking deep and labored breaths as he answered, "We are making our way down the mountain now. It's going to be cutting it close but I think that we can make it."

Gina answered with a deadly tone to her voice, "Make sure you are clear in that time frame because if you are not, that Yeti is going to be running out of the valley just as you two are reaching the base the of the mountain."

Axe breathed hard into the radio, "Copy that!"

Gina put her radio back into her pocket and relayed her conversation with Axe to Henry. Henry nodded and said, "Alright, let's push it and get the hell out of here."

The two snowmobiles continued to rocket through the prehistoric valley. Far to their left, they saw another herd of mammoths walking by. Gina briefly hoped that Yukon would take the opportunity to prey on the mammoths, but in her heart she knew that nothing would distract the Yeti from pursuing her and Thu-Ca. As she thought about Thu-Ca, she looked over to see the baby quietly sleeping in Jun-Tuk's arms. She could see that the old man was a natural with infants. She then looked over at Henry and smiled as she thought of what an excellent father her husband would be. Gina's happy thoughts faded away when she heard Yukon roar again, reminding her that the monster was not far behind them.

Several minutes later, the valley pass came into view. Gina picked up her radio and called the demolition experts, "Axe, are you two clear of the danger zone?"

Axe could barely talk because he was breathing so hard, "We... need about... five more minutes... You guys have to clear a mile out of the pass as well before we can cause the avalanche."

Gina spoke into her radio, "Copy that. See you guys soon." She yelled over to Henry, "We need to be a mile out of the valley before they can cause the avalanche!"

Henry nodded as he aimed his snowmobile directly at the quickly approaching valley pass. The few minutes that it took to reach the valley pass seemed to drag on for an eternity, but the snowmobiles finally cleared the opening between the mountains. They maneuvered around the rocks at the valley pass and then they continued to move in a straight line away from the pass and toward the campsite. It took them several more minutes to clear the mile marker. When they reached a safe distance, they stopped their snowmobiles and turned around so that they could see the pass. As Gina was looking back toward the pass, she could see the colossal form of Yukon sprinting toward it. She yelled into her radio, "Now! Blow the charges now!"

There was a deafening explosion and Gina watched as tons of snow, ice, and rock were thrown into the air. Yukon was entering the valley pass just as the explosion went off. The Yeti ignored the devastation occurring around him and he continued to run toward Gina. The anthropologist held her breath as the avalanche made its way down the mountain. Yukon was still running at full speed and Gina thought for a moment that the incredible beast would actually outrun the avalanche. She closed her eyes and said a silent prayer to a higher power that her baby would be saved from the monster.

She opened her eyes to see the avalanche come crashing down at the base of the mountain behind Yukon. The Yeti was moving at an unbelievable speed but the wall of snow and ice behind him was moving even faster. Gina watched as Yukon was overtaken by the rush of snow like a child trying to exit the ocean only to have a wave come crashing down on top of him.

Yukon's body was tossed and turned as the avalanche used up the last of its strength. Yukon vanished under the snow as the avalanche came to a halt less than a half mile from Gina, Henry, Jun-Tuk, and the baby. When the snow finally stopped moving, Henry climbed off his snowmobile, ran over to Gina, and hugged her. He whispered into her ear, "It's over. It's finally over."

Gina kissed her husband and said, "Henry, I have something to tell you." Gina smiled and then there was a loud roar behind them. Gina turned around to see Yukon climbing out of the snow that had buried him. The Yeti walked through the deep snow of the avalanche then he started running toward to Gina and Thu-Ca.

No one wasted time talking; instead they all jumped onto their snowmobiles. Henry climbed onto one snowmobile and Gina and Jun-Tuk climbed onto the second vehicle. Once they were moving, Gina called out over her radio, "Base camp, this is Gina Murella, come in! Do you copy?"

The familiar voice of Dana Summers came back over the radio, "Gina, you are alive! Is the valley sealed off? We heard the explosion and the avalanche."

"Yes, but the Yeti managed to make it out of the valley. He is still in chasing us. How is the evacuation going?"

Dana voice came back filled with fear, "We are not able to evacuate! There is a large pod of orcas off the coast. They have herded hundreds of seals to shore. The seals are occupying the only stretch of beach for miles that does not have jagged underwater rocks leading up to the shoreline. The transport boats can't come ashore with all of those seals blocking the way. Those seals are keeping us trapped here and the orcas aren't letting them leave."

Gina's worst nightmare was coming true. She was leading Yukon back to camp where he would massacre everyone in sight and there was nowhere for them to escape to. She looked behind her to see that they had gained a little ground on Yukon. Gina pulled her snowmobile to a stop. She turned around to Jun-Tuk. "Jun-Tuk, you have been watching us use these machines. Do you think that you could operate this machine and hold the baby?"

The old man nodded. "When I was young I could row a canoe on the great ocean and hold my daughter on my lap. I think that I can operate this dog-less sled and still hold the child."

Gina was instructing Jun-Tuk on how to operate the snowmobile when Henry pulled up beside her. "What are you doing? That monster is right behind us!"

Gina ignored Henry and finished showing Jun-Tuk how to operate the machine. She then pointed to the west. "Go that way and you will find the other people that we came here with."

Yukon was less than a hundred feet behind them as Jun-Tuk took off to the west and Gina climbed onto Henry's snowmobile. She screamed, "Go straight ahead toward the ocean!"

Henry did as she said then he yelled, "We are almost out of gas! Why aren't we heading for the transport boats?"

Gina took a deep breath. "The transport boats can't come ashore. A large pod of orcas have forced a massive amount of seals onto the beach. There are taking up the only landing area where it is not too rocky for the transport boats to land."

Henry nodded. "We're trapped and you don't want anyone else to die." He spoke with as much courage as he could muster. "Don't worry. I won't let that monster take you alive."

Gina hugged her husband. "I love you, Henry. You are everything that I could have asked for in a husband. Don't worry, our journey together doesn't end here. In fact, it's only beginning." The line of seals and the ocean came into view. The sun was just starting to set to the west and it cast an orange glow over the gathered seals and the ocean behind them. The scene was one of the most beautiful things that Gina had ever beheld. Then she looked at the thick black fins circling in the waters just off the coast. She whispered into Henry's ear, "Let me off just in front of the seals and then head down the beach a little way. Yukon will follow me."

They had reached the seals and Henry pulled the snowmobile to a stop. Gina climbed off and quickly kissed her husband through their ski masks. She turned to see Yukon less than fifty feet behind them. She handed Henry the radio and yelled, "Go!"

Tears welled up in Henry's eyes. There was so much that he wanted to say to his beloved wife but she had said that their journey together didn't end here. Henry loved his wife and he trusted her. As he drove down the beach, he knew that he would have the chance to tell her everything that he felt.

Gina took one look at Henry and the she started wading into the massed seals. The animals were making all kinds of sounds and climbing over each other in a panic as Yukon ran toward them from the beach and the orcas circled in the water. The panicked seals finally decided to take their chances in the ocean rather than have Yukon slaughter them, and as one, they rushed into the frigid waters of the ocean. As the seals dashed into the freezing water, Gina followed them.

Her body felt like a thousand knives had pierced her skin as the cold ocean water attacked her body. The pain only lasted for a few seconds before her entire body went numb. She could feel herself starting to blackout, but when she saw the enraged Yukon step into the surf, she forced herself to stay awake and go deeper into the water.

When Henry saw Gina go into the water, he grabbed his radio. "Dana, this is Henry, we are going to need a Sno-Cat with a hyperthermia kit one mile north of base camp ASAP!"

Dana voice came back rushed, "Roger that. We are climbing aboard and will be heading out in less than one minute."

Henry replied, "Please hurry! Push that thing as fast as it will go!"

Gina was nearly in shoulder deep water when Yukon had caught up to her. He was reaching down to grab her, but once they saw the orcas, the seals panicked again and swam back to shore. A fleeing seal bumped into Gina and knocked her away from Yukon's claw. Gina tumbled through the icy water and out of the corner of her eye, she saw a thick black and white form collide with Yukon's leg. The collision caused the Yeti to lose his footing and fall into the water. The Yeti rolled over to see the jaws of an orca wide open and coming for him. Yukon howled in pain as the Orca closed its jaws on his arm and shoulder. Blood poured out of the Yeti and it turned the ocean around him red. Yukon dug his free claw into the whale's side. Then, in another show of his immense strength the Yeti stood up, lifted the orca out of the water, and slammed it down into the surf. The orca crashed into the water then it rolled over a few times and headed back out to sea. Yukon roared at the fleeing orca and Gina watched as a second orca crashed into Yukon's leg and knocked him into the water again. This time the orca had grabbed Yukon's leg and the powerful oceanic predator was fighting to pull Yukon out into the ocean. Gina had been trying to swim back to shore but her freezing body had stopped responding. She saw a seal swim past her and she was content to let herself slip beneath the waves when she felt strong arms wrap around her. Henry pulled her out of the water and said, "Like you said, our journey together isn't over yet. " He pulled her head out of the water and she watched as Yukon continually struck the orca in the face until it let him go.

By the time that Yukon had managed to free himself, the orca had drug the mighty Yeti into waist-deep water. The orca circled back out into deeper water then it and one of its fellow pod members swam toward Yukon like living torpedoes. Henry pulled Gina ashore and through chattering teeth she said, "Orcas form families... to attack one is to attack them all... Like Jun-Tuk said... The Yeti is the greatest predator on land but the orca is the greatest predator in the sea. Yukon is out of his element and outnumbered. This is one fight that he won't win."

Gina and Henry watched as one of the orcas slammed into Yukon's hip. The whale dug its teeth into Yukon's thigh and the force of the attack spun Yukon around so that he was facing the shore. Yukon threw his arms out and roared in defiance, and when he did so, a second orca leapt out of the water and clamped its jaws around Yukon's arm. The Yeti didn't roar in pain. He looked silently at Gina with eyes that were filled with sadness from loss and betrayal. The Yeti only looked at Gina for a second, and for all of the rage that she had seen within Yukon's eyes, his last look of sadness would stay with her for the rest of her life. Gina held Yukon's gaze for that brief second before the orcas pulled him under the frigid waves. A pool of blood gushed out of the water where Yukon had gone under. Gina and Henry sat freezing to death on the beach where they waited for several long minutes. When Yukon did not surface Gina said, "Now it's over."

Henry hugged her. "Now all we have to do is not die from freezing to death before Dana gets here."

Gina looked at the now almost fully set sun as it sent the last vestiges of its orange light across the ocean. She looked at the hundreds of beautiful seals around them. Then she looked at the frozen wasteland that had become like a second home to her and Henry over the last several years. She realized that this is exactly where she wanted to be. She couldn't feel Henry holding her but she tried to snuggle closer to him. She forced her frozen face to smile and she said, "You can't freeze to death here, Daddy. Your baby is going to need you."

A huge smile slowly formed on Henry's face. "My baby! You mean...?" Gina nodded and Henry hugged his freezing wife as hard as he could. To the left of the couple, the last rays of the sun dipped into ocean, and as they did so, the lights of Dana's Sno-Cat came into view.

EPILOGUE

Six months later

Gina and Henry were sitting in their house in New Jersey. They had nearly managed to put the events of what had occurred in Antarctica behind them. Thanks to Dana, both of them had survived nearly freezing to death after plunging into the icy ocean waters. Most importantly, the baby in Gina's womb was also unaffected by her exposure to the extreme cold. After several hours at the campsite, the standoff between the orcas and the seals finally came to its only possible end. The seals' hunger finally forced them to take to the ocean where some of them lost their lives to the orcas. When the orcas had eaten their fill, the seals finally cleared off the beach. With the seals gone, the transport boats were able to come to shore and then to return everyone to the ship. Prior to leaving Antarctica, Gina and Henry saw Jun-Tuk one last time. The old man had asked to raise Thu-Ca as his grandson. He felt that if his daughter had cared for the infant for several weeks after he was born, he was a much Shunu's son as he was Wen-Ku's. Jun-Tuk was happy to raise the infant as his grandson. He hugged Gina and Henry and thanked them for helping him to ease his sorrow from the loss of his daughter by helping to him to find his grandson. He also thanked them for helping to free his people from the reign of the Yeti. Jun-Tuk felt that by returning to his tribe with the infant, he could prove to them that the Yeti was not a god because no human could wrest an infant from the clutches of a divine being. Jun-Tuk also felt that those who still believed in the Yeti's godhood would abandon those beliefs as time passed and the Yeti did not return to their village. With a final goodbye to Gina and Henry, Jun-Tuk took Thu-Ca and headed back to the village and out of the young couple's lives forever.

Once Gina and Henry had recovered from their ordeal, they radioed Princeton about the events that occurred during their expedition. The fallout from the expedition was extensive. While Gina and Henry were found to be clear of any legally responsible for the deaths of the people who died in the valley, the personal toll on both of them was tremendous. Through a mutual agreement with Princeton, both Gina and Henry resigned from their positions at the university.

After much deliberation between the scientific community and the United States government, it was decided that the valley itself, as well as the Quinic tribe, would be put under the jurisdiction of the United Nations. No independent nation would be able to study the unique valley without UN approval. Once the legal matters regarding the valley were taken care of, there was the long list of funerals to attend. Gina and Henry still held themselves responsible for the deaths of their students and they attend as many of the funerals of those who had died as the families would allow them to. While most of the families did not blame Gina and Henry for the deaths of their loved ones, there were several who felt the two professors were negligent in their duties. A lawsuit was filed, but since everyone who went into the valley volunteered to do so, the case was dismissed. Gina and Henry still felt as if they had to do something to honor those who died during their expedition and they worked with Princeton to construct a memorial on the campus for those who died in the valley. The construction of the memorial helped Gina and Henry to ease their minds and to mentally move on from the deaths of their students.

Once word of the events that took place reached the public, Gina was offered several book deals and even a movie contract for her story. She was told that she would make millions by taking any one of the offers but her conscious would not let her accept money for an event that had seen the deaths of so many people.

She and Henry were both able to find new jobs teaching at a local community college. They were teaching first and second year college students in positions where field research would not be an aspect of their duties. Gina's pregnancy was going well and she had decided to work as long as she could prior to giving birth. While their lives were significantly different than they were before the expedition, both husband and wife were happy with their new lives. They also both looked forward to continuing their journey together, not only as husband and wife, but also as mother and father.

Gina and Henry kept in touch with both Dana Summers and Tony Gordon. It took Gordon several months of physical therapy to return his arm to where he could use it again. In that time, the relationship between he and Dana continued to grow. Aside from the fact that Gordon was no longer able use a rifle due to the damage to his arm, he had also decided that he had enough death for one lifetime. The former hunter moved to Wyoming where he became a park ranger at Yellowstone National Park. The former hunter now took the time to help people appreciate the diverse animals which inhabited our planet. Dana Summers followed Gordon to Wyoming where she opened up her own medical practice. They had moved in together and it did not seem long before the two of them were officially engaged.

Antarctica, The Valley

Clouds had blanketed the sky as another blizzard made its way over the massive mountain tops that surrounded the huge valley. The snow was just starting to fall as a lone Yeti walked along the eastern-most slope of the mountains. Until recently, the Yeti had been the alpha male of his family and he ruled over all that he saw. The Yeti had grown older and a younger male had challenged his position as alpha male. After a long and fierce battle, the older Yeti was defeated. He was forced to leave his family and to become an outcast. His family mainly stayed in the western half of the valley and now he was forced to wander the eastern border of the valley alone. Being a social creature, the Yeti longed for the companionship that had once been offered by his family but he was not able to find that companionship within the valley.

The Yeti had taken to wandering the eastern end of the valley and looking for the ever-wandering mammoth herds to hunt. He was walking along the slope of mountain when he saw something different in the landscape ahead of him. The curious Yeti approached the oddity and examined it. The rest of the valley was encased by a mountain range that was packed tightly together forming a wall of impenetrable rock but here was different. Here it looked as if there was an opening in the wall where the snow and loose boulders had fallen down and filled in the opening. The Yeti stared at the now filled-in opening. He knew that there was nothing that could ease his loneliness within the valley but he wondered if perhaps there were others like him outside of the valley. The Yeti walked to the snow and ice that filled in the opening out of the valley. The beast picked up one of the large boulders and he tossed it aside.

The Yeti had no concept of time. He did not comprehend that he could spend the rest of his life moving boulders and still he may not clear enough boulders to make it out of the valley. He only knew that he wanted to make it to the other side of the opening to see if there were others like him there. The Yeti picked another rock and tossed it aside. He then continued to move boulders with a grim determination to keep digging until he was able to find someone who could ease his isolation.

THE END

CHECK OUT OTHER GREAT DINOSAUR THRILLERS

THE VALLEY
by Rick Jones

In a dystopian future, a self-contained valley in Argentina serves as the 'far arena' for those convicted of a crime. Inside the Valley: carnivorous dinosaurs generated from preserved DNA. The goal: cross the Valley to get to the Gates of Freedom. The chance of survival: no one has ever completed the journey. Convicted of crimes with little or no merit, Ben Peyton and others must battle their way across fields filled with the world's deadliest apex predators in order to reach salvation. All the while the journey is caught on cameras and broadcast to the world as a reality show, the deaths and killings real, the macabre appetite of the audience needing to be satiated as Ben Peyton leads his team to escape not only from a legal system that's more interested in entertainment than in justice, but also from the predators of the Valley.

JURASSIC DEAD
by Rick Chesler & David Sakmyster

An Antarctic research team hoping to study microbial organisms in an underground lake discovers something far more amazing: perfectly preserved dinosaur corpses. After one thaws and wakes ravenously hungry, it becomes apparent that death, like life, will find a way.
Environmental activist Alex Ramirez, son of the expedition's paleontologist, came to Antarctica to defend the organisms from extinction, but soon learns that it is the human race that needs protecting.

CHECK OUT OTHER GREAT DINOSAUR THRILLERS

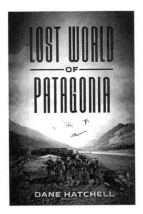

LOST WORLD OF PATAGONIA
by Dane Hatchell

An earthquake opens a path to a land hidden for millions of years. Under the guise of finding cryptid animals, Ace Corporation sends Alex Klasse, a Cryptozoologist and university professor, his associates, and a band of mercenaries to explore the Lost World of Patagonia. The crew boards a nuclear powered All-Terrain Tracked Carrier and takes a harrowing ride into the unknown.

The expedition soon discovers prehistoric creatures still exist. But the dangers won't prevent a sub-team from leaving the group in search of rare jewels. Tensions run high as personalities clash, and man proves to be just as deadly as the dinosaurs that roam the countryside.

Lost World of Patagonia is a prehistoric thriller filled with murder, mayhem, and savage dinosaur action.

SAVAGE ISLAND
by Alan Spencer

Somewhere in the Atlantic Ocean, an uncharted island has been used for the illegal dumping of chemicals and pollutants for years by Globo Corp's. Private investigator Pierce Range will learn plenty about the evil conglomerate when Susan Branch, an environmentalist from The Green Project, hires him to join the expedition to save her kidnapped father from Globo Corp's evil hands.

Things go to hell in a hurry once the team reaches the island. The bloodthirsty dinosaurs and voracious cannibals are only the beginning of the fight for survival. Pierce must unlock the mysteries surrounding the toxic operation and somehow remain in one piece to complete the rescue mission.

Ratchet up the body count, because this mission will leave the killing floor soaked in blood and chewed up corpses. When the insane battle ends, will there by anybody left alive to survive Savage Island?

Made in the USA
Middletown, DE
20 January 2016